Annette Israel

New
Tires

2020 © Annette Israel

New Tires

Soft Cover ISBN: 978-1-09834-918-9

eBook ISBN: 978-1-09834-919-6

AUTHOR'S NOTE

ACKNOWLEDGEMENTS

My thanks to First Reader Marquette Baker.

Special thanks to beloved friends: Kathy and Tim, Jeanine, and Nancy.

DEDICATION

For G

CONTENTS

Chapter One: *Into the Store*   1

Chapter Two: *The Waiting Room*   7

Chapter Three: *Free to go — Free to Stay*   56

Chapter Four: *Time to Go*   82

CHAPTER ONE

Into the Store

I woke up this morning feeling like a depressed pineapple. That's the best way to describe it. And, to weigh me down even more, among other things, my beater-car has to have new tires. Today. I don't think that the old ones will last another week. I'd hoped to ditch the whole car before I had to break down and buy new tires, but I can't drive another day on slicks. And, for that matter, who wants to buy a beater on slicks anyway? They're having a sale on tires this whole week and that makes it all a little easier for me to stomach.

After two pots of coffee and a stale blueberry muffin, I venture out the backdoor. I'm still not feeling any better. There was not one good thing on the news this morning. That's something I can get even more down about. I can get down on us. I can get down on humanity for all of the mean-spirited things we do to each other. I can always tell when the news isn't going to be good. And that's an almost every day thing. Sickness here, assault there, name-calling, criticism of every-thing and every-one. I guess I'm no better because I'm criticizing the news. I don't know if that's accurate or not. But I don't care. Today I'm questioning if I know anything at all. That's what it feels like.

It's one of those first gray autumn days and it looks like serious rain is headed our way. The news said that, and, by the looks of it, the weather lady is correct. Even though she's wrong, a lot, she's probably correct today. Sometimes I want to tell her how wrong she is, but how? She's on television and here I sit. This doesn't make me any happier. Anyway, there aren't herds of cars on the roads as I head out and that makes my trip, and my upcoming loss of bucks, a tad less awful.

It's my last day of errands on the old skins. After all of the errands that included stops at the post office, the bank, and gathering a few needed items, here I am standing with a plastic bag of groceries, ready to go in the house, and the bag is cleverly in the process of ripping from bottom to top. I'll be able to balance it all, I hope, to make the short jaunt into the house. I close the car door and can't help but notice the tires even though the bag continues to rip. Both the bag and the tires beg for my attention. The old, cracked and near-gray skins look even squattier just since this morning. It's time. They've gotta go.

I think I've squandered a good part of this day. Sometimes doing that just seems appropriate and feels good too. Who is making that guess but me? I'm my own accuser and my own cheerleader. But I don't care which one I am today. It's only me.

It doesn't take me long to stash things where they need to be stashed, or, close enough to where they belong, and back out I go to head to the tire place. It's not really a tire store. It's a big department store. I'm pulling into the parking lot now. I'll just park out front and walk through the store part of the department store that sells just about anything you can think of besides tires. There's lots of stuff on sale today. Sheets are on sale and tools are on sale. Even kid's toys are on sale. I think it's a store-wide sale and maybe for the whole week. But all I need are my tires.

Up the aisle a few feet in front of me I see a huge roll of bubble-wrap attached to some sort of contraption overhead. Nothing makes your day like bubble-wrap. I'm going right over there to pop a bunch of them. I look from side-to-side to see if anyone is watching. A woman springs out of the shoe aisle. So, I dart to the side and grab the price tag on a shoe, not even my size, pretending I'm interested in that shoe…and not the bubble-wrap. This woman has the same plan I do. I can tell. But I'm closer. She smiles at me, flicking her eyes down to the floor. She's perhaps a little embarrassed that she's been caught in the pending act. I'm a little sorry that she missed her turn. But I got here first. She scurries on down to the women's wear section. She's pretending, too, just like me. I'm watching until I know she's gone for good.

I don't remember the day I learned to pop bubble-wrap. Do you remember *your* first time? I don't remember the first time I ever did it. But I can't remember *not* popping bubbles. I don't know if it's truly fun or just habit now.

I'm at the huge roll of wrap. I reach out to grasp the clear sheet only to find the full-width, about six-feet across, has all popped bubbles. Every bubble has been popped, not only on the full-width, but from the bottom of the sheet to as far up as the tallest human could reach. Every single one of them—popped. A store clerk probably used one of those rolling-ladder-gizmos to reach the highest bubbles. There were no bubbles left for me.

Don't you just know that a psychologist would tell us that there is some deep, dark reason why we pop the bubbles and that there is an even darker reason to explain that little rush of something that we get at the moment of popping? That psychologist would tell us, "Freud says…" and then when you leave his office, he will open up his desk drawer and pop the last of the bubbles from a sheet he found in the mail room that morning. I offer no excuses. I love to pop the bubbles. There is a technique that we all use: We pinch each bubble between our thumb and forefinger. You hear that wonderful little cracking sound and feel that resistance and then that nice little glob of mush and flatness between your fingertips. And then you move on to the next bubble. I know some people who roll them up and twist the whole shebang at once. It sounds like a mini Gatling gun. But that's not my style. I always pop them one-at-a-time. When did each of us learn to do this? I think it might just be emulation, and never was an actual lesson. It's kind of like how wild turkeys follow each other but have no clue why they are going anywhere at all, or where they are all headed, yet, they seem to be on a mission that matters to them. Something about that is important to turkeys. Something about the bubbles is important to us.

Crap. I just realized that I'm walking through the store, and the auto-service part is way in the back of the huge building. They will ask me to bring my car up to the big garage doors. This means I will have to walk all the way back through the store, get my car from the front lot, and then drive it all the way behind the store where I should have gone when I got here. Stupid of me. It's even stupider that I'm not turning around now at this point to go back and get the car. It's almost as if I expect my car to appear on its own in the proper place by some miraculous means. Of course, there is that stupid part of me that thinks there might be another option. But what other option *could* there be? I know there isn't another option, but I keep walking to the service desk anyway.

Sure enough.

"Just bring your car up to door number three," the service clerk says.

4

Back through the store I go. I choose another aisle rather than have to look at the popped bubble-wrap and become depressed about that all over again.

Hanging out now in the lobby of the main entrance to the store are a woman and a small ringlet-curled girl. I think they might be waiting for a ride home. The little girl, I'd guess to be five or six, is cradling a pink blanket in her arms. She is right in front of the door. So, I feel as though I have to say *something*. In preparation, I smile down at the youngster who proudly pulls back a corner of the blanket to display her baby as her mother guides her away from the door so that I can leave the building. I'm looking down at the dolly in the blanket and what I see is a larger-than-my-forearm, green as can be–zucchini, all comfortably and tenderly wrapped up in the pink blanket. For a few moments, I'm frozen in place. What do I say? So, instead of trying to make a comment, I smile instead, and nod, and out the door I go. Did I really just see a zucchini all wrapped up in a baby blanket?

I'm not sure if I should laugh though I want to burst out in hysterics. I doubt that would have been appropriate when I was in the lobby. It may have devasted the tyke. So, I'm glad I didn't laugh when the baby was revealed. And the urge to laugh has simmered down now. That urge has been replaced with questions swirling all around in my brain. Is that what I truly saw? Maybe I only *thought* I saw a zucchini. Why a zucchini? How did that happen?

I wonder what the baby's name is.

I mount the old clunker and coast all the way around to the back of the huge building and park it in front of door number three, just as I was told to do, just as I knew I should have done. I'm still thinking about the baby in the blanket. I really want to know her name. I go through the people door of the garage and hand over the keys to the clerk.

Zoey? Amanda? Kelly?

"We'll bring it in when we're ready," the cheerful clerk says. He's smiling. He's nineteen. This is his first job. I can tell. He didn't watch the news today. Maybe he did but it didn't add to wrecking his day like it did mine. But I'm older. Lots of things can wreck my day. He's just plain old happy. A happy nineteen-year-old, just starting his adult life.

"You can wait in the waiting room," he says, big sincere smile. He's proud of the job he's doing. I can tell.

CHAPTER TWO

The Waiting-Room

The Waiting-Room is actually quite nice. There are tan vinyl sofas along the walls and a few brown chairs that sort of match the sofas. There is a table in the center of the room with the appropriate magazines arranged on it: *People, Women's Day, National Geographic, Sportsman* and, of course, a newspaper. There are a few people in here too. I first notice a very large Black guy sitting in the corner. His head is down and he's reading one of the magazines. I don't know which one. Across the room is an old couple. They are sitting close to each other. The old woman has her feet crossed at the ankles. She's wearing pink track shoes. The old man sits with his knees cast off to the sides, and he has a walking stick propped against the sofa next to him. They've been married more than sixty years. I can tell. I sit on the sofa sort of in the middle. No one is saying anything. This doesn't bother me. I don't have to be talking every minute. But when I need to, I can have a conversation with an elm tree. I'm also a good listener. Old Man and Old Woman are sitting so close to each other and not talking to Big Black Guy because they are afraid of him. I can tell. They are, at least, uncomfortable in his presence. Old Woman lifts her eyes every now and then to catch a glimpse of Big Black Guy. She does this in a subtle way to avoid any chance of making eye contact with him. But Big Black Guy's focus is on the pages of his magazine.

None of the magazines interest me. I'd prefer to paw through *Entertainment* but there isn't one. So, I'm just sitting here looking bored. There will be a wait because my beater is still outside of door number three waiting its turn to come in. I don't know what stage Old Man and Old Woman's vehicle is at. I don't know where Big Black Guy's car is. We're all here for new tires. It's not like you get a whole new vehicle when you crack open your wallet for new tires. We won't even get new wheels. You just get new skins that will take you the next miles you have to go and wherever the upcoming journeys may take you. So, just like everyone else, I wait my turn.

After about ten minutes, Big Black Guy stands up. Oh my. He's over six-feet-tall. He is *way* over six-feet-tall. I would guess him to be about six-foot-five maybe six-foot-six. He stretches his long arms out in front of him. His biceps are the size of school buses. No wonder the old couple is afraid of him. He thrusts his hands into his pockets, some kind of work uniform pants, and he jingles keys. The uniform pants look like he probably works as a janitor. I can tell. He's a janitor. Big Black Guy has a nice pocketful of keys that he's flinging around. My dad used to do that. It bugs the crap out of everyone but no one ever says, "Stop it! You're making me crazy with that!" We just let them jingle. And we try not to visibly cringe. Then we forget all about it until the next time. And there will be a next time. Key jinglers are life-long enthusiasts.

Big Black Guy pivots to look out the large bay window into the service area. I stand up now, too, but I'm nowhere near as impressive. I walk over to the window and stretch for lack of anything better to do. Three of the workers out in the garage are standing around a large pallet on which they've stacked about thirty car batteries. They are wrapping and wrapping the whole thing with plastic wrap. Around and around they go with the wrapping, like they are making one huge sandwich wrap.

"What are they doing?" I ask. But I don't look at him.

"They have to wrap and dispose of batteries a certain way 'ccordin' to codes to make sure there's no leakage of battery fluid," Big Black Guy says.

I don't say anything for a few seconds. I'm sort of pretending that I know that. I kind of wish I had a few keys in a pocket to jingle.

"Which car is yours?" I finally say.

"That pickup with all of the fishin' gear in the back."

Well...*he* knows there's fishing gear in the back of the truck. But I just see some crates and metal cans poking up that don't display any signs of fishing. Funny how when we know something so familiar to us, we assume that the rest of the world gets it. I don't see any fishing gear. I'll just have to take his word for it. But I still want to chat with him.

"You fish a lot?"

"Every chance I get, often as I can get out there. Been at it my whole life. Started fishin' with my Gramps when I was five."

"Where do you go?"

"Headed north. Got a little cottage right on a lake and there's a mess a fish in that lake. Good eatin' fish," he says with a wink and a broad smile. He's jingling his keys briskly now.

"Sounds like you had a lot of fun and learned a lot," I say, but I'm thinking it's a weird human trait that we feel a need to talk to a stranger when we've nothing better to do. It's like we *have* to be talking. We have to do that to reaffirm that we're human and that for some reason we need to express that we're important enough to have something to say and a reason for being. Why is it that we don't just sit there in total silence and be content with only our own thoughts? But we don't.

"I got the dang-best memories of those days. And Gramps was good. He was the best. I remember one summer when I was just learnin' to fish. We're out on a long dock. I thought it was a mile-long dock but it wasn't no more'n probably forty-feet and Gramps'd come and put a worm on the hook because I didn't want to do it. He'd come all the way out onto the dock and put my worm on. Then I'd catch me a fish and try to reel it in. 'Gramps,' I'd scream, 'I caught one.' Gramps'd come runnin' out onto the dock and reel the fish in and take it off the hook. It was just a little bluegill, so we'd toss him back in. Gramps'd bait the hook again and he'd no sooner walk back across the dock and sit down with his newspaper, in his chair, and I'd be screamin' that I caught one again. Back he'd come flyin' down the dock to help me with the fish and back he'd go. This went on for 'bout seven, maybe eight trips, and finally when Gramps came out, he said, 'I think you're catching the same little fish over and over.' Then I started to bawl like a baby cuz I felt sorry for that poor little fish. Gramps picked me up and told me that the little fish was okay, but we needed to give him a rest. I think he meant more that *Gramps* needed a rest. But it was a good day. He taught me everything you need to know 'bout fishin' over the years. He was proud that I learned to fish." The key jingling continues. A little slower.

We resumed watching the battery wrappers. It's good that *someone* is wrapping batteries. It gives us something to look at.

"Excuse me," Old Man says, "you said you have a cottage?"

Old Man and Old Woman are now feeling that the large Black man isn't going to chop them into little old pieces and roast them over a campfire. Their fear of the big fellow is dwindling. I can tell.

Big Black Guy and I turn to look at the couple.

"Yep," Big Black Guy says.

"Do you know anything about raccoons? We have a cottage, too, and this family of raccoons gets into the garbage no matter how I tie down the lids and no matter how much weight I put on the lids. They still manage to get in, and then they scatter the garbage that they don't want all over the yard. Any ideas what I can do with them?"

Big Black Guy takes three strides across the room and sits back down on the sofa closer to Old Man. I take six steps to join them. I counted.

"I'll tell you what to do," Big Black Guy says as he leans a little closer to Old Man. "You gonna have to keep the garbage inside somewhere or get a can that has a lock on it. Or, you might have to trap 'em," he says shaking his head. "You get yourself a live trap. Don't be lettin' no one trap 'em and kill 'em or shoot 'em. They mean no harm. They just wanna eat like we all do."

Old Man nods. "We don't want to kill them either." He smirks. "I just want them to find another restaurant."

All four of us in The Waiting-Room now share in the relieved sense of levity and this isn't because what Old Man said was that funny. We just needed to release some awkwardness that we've all been clutching. So, we're all laughing, but politely, because we don't know each other. At least there is some common ground where we might not feel so awkward sitting in silence pretending to read magazines that we have no interest in or clearing our throats while we stare at our shoes.

"I do have a good story 'bout a raccoon though," Big Black Guy says. He leans yet closer, more into the tale he's about to tell. He tosses his head back and squints, like we do in belief that this will help us to think better.

Since we do have to pass this time in some manner, hearing a story about a raccoon will accomplish that for us. It beats the alternative—which is nothing.

"It was back 'bout fifteen years ago," Big Black Guy says, "when I still worked for the County Road Commission," he says. "I was *the* Road Commissioner, head of the whole agency, but every now and then I would work the road just to stay in touch with my crew and my guys. So, one night I was out with the crew and my partner and I was comin' in from a job 'bout midnight. I'm drivin', okay? Right in the road in front of us was this little critter runnin'...thinkin' he could outrun a county truck. 'Hit it,' my partner says. 'Not hittin' no critter, man,' I told him. I pulled over and jumped out of the truck. By then, the little thing, tiny raccoon, was crouched on the gravel, shakin' that little body from cold and fear. He let me pick him up. I stuffed him inside my coat and zipped him up and got back in the truck. I look over at my partner and his eyes all big and rollin' back in his head and he's laughin' at me like a fool. 'So now we got a raccoon with us in the truck. What are you going to do with it, eat it?' he says. 'Not gonna eat no baby raccoon,' I says. 'I'll figure out a way to feed him and then let him go,' Yeah, I told him good.

"That little critter snuggled up tight against my chest inside my coat and never moved. I could feel him breathin'. I could feel him shakin', and then I could feel him startin' to get warmed up and startin' to relax."

"What did you do with him?" Old Woman asks.

"He was no bigger than this," Big Black Guy says as he circles the center of his palm. "He fit right here. I named him Matthew, after the Apostle. I had to get one of my little girl's doll bottles and fill it with warm milk to keep feedin' him. Matthew got his milk from that toy bottle. I had to take him to work with me, in my coat, in a shirt pocket, and I'd take him out every hour and let him suck on the bottle. I kept the bottle in my pocket to keep it warm. Oh, Lordy, how I got razzed about takin' Matthew to work with me."

Big Black Guy chuckles and smiles. Remembering. "When he wasn't all tucked in and wrapped in my shirt, I kept him in a towel in my desk drawer. He never tried to climb out. Not once. He thought it was a fine nest."

I see that Old Woman has tears in her eyes. She and Old Man are smiling that soft, tender smile we make at times when we're thinking… and…changing our thoughts. *He's not so scary after all.*

"Matthew grew and grew and he was eatin' fish outta my hand," Big Black Guy says, looking down. He laughs and shakes his head. "He liked perch the best, just like me. I knew I had to let him go back to the woods. So, one day, I drove my truck back out to where I found him. I took him out of my coat, he was almost a full-size raccoon then, and I walked out to the woods. I set him on a nice big maple stump, and we said our goodbyes. When I got back to my truck, I turned to have a last look. Matthew was gone. Never seen him again. That's my raccoon story."

We're not saying anything. We know that this was a special bond that Big Black Guy had shared with the little creature. I certainly didn't expect a story like that. Big Black Guy's head is down and he's smiling a gentle smile while looking at his hand. I know he sees the raccoon, little Matthew, right there on his palm again. I can tell.

13

"Well," Old Woman says, "you picked a good name for him. I'm sure the real Matthew is very honored."

Big Black Guy smiles and nods as he looks at Old Woman. "Yeah, I think you might be right 'bout that," he says. "Matthew was a good name for him."

"God loaned Matthew, for a time, to a man He loves," Old Woman says.

Big Black smiles and nods a thank-you.

The Waiting-Room door opens and in blows a woman I would guess to be about twenty-five. She has super short black hair. It looks like at least two hairdressers chopped her hair with several razors, all at the same time, and then sprayed it stiff with cement. It suits her. I like it. She's probably the only one who could pull off that style. She glances around, ready to pick her spot on a sofa. She walks across the room and plops down.

"Hi," she says. We all say, "Hi" right back.

"Is everyone here getting new tires?" She asks. "It's quite a savings today?"

We're all murmuring at the same time. We're all bobbing our heads up and down and smiling along with it. This reminds me of bobbleheads that ride along in your car on your dashboard. A bunch of them though. A herd of bobbleheads all bobbing at the same time but not in time with each other. Just bobbing along to our individual rhythm and answer to the question.

The new woman slips off a light sweater. Everyone is staring at her now but trying not to stare in a manner that she can see. This woman is plastered in tattoos. There is no skin without ink. She is covered in bright-colored tattoos from her neck down to her chest and up and down both arms. She opens up a small purse and sorts through some cards. When each of us has assessed the fullness of the ink-work, we all turn away and return to doing what we've been doing in The Waiting-Room—waiting. I'm sure all of those tattoos have meaning and I'm sure she didn't get them all at one time. I mean, don't they hurt? I think they look hideous and it further wrecks my day to see a young woman mutilate herself like that.

Young Clerk opens the door and pops his head in. He's not smiling.

"They just issued a tornado warning," he says. "It's store policy that I can't let you leave. This is a safe room. I'll be bringing some other customers in here too. I'll make some fresh coffee in a few."

Young Clerk backs out and another woman walks in. She's slim and she looks fit. Could she be an athlete of some sort? She removes her glasses and rubs her eyes, nods a quick thank you to Young Clerk and then she takes up her position on the sofa that faces the door. She looks at each of us, purses her lips and lifts her eyebrows. "Looks like we might be here for a while," she says. "There are all kinds of threats and warnings and watches for several counties."

"It was pouring when I came in?" Tattoos says.

Tattoos speaks in the latest version of the acquired national vernacular. She ends every sentence as a question. I'm told this is called Upspeak. I hope I don't do it. At least I hope I don't do it a *lot* anyway. I try to catch myself and stop it before I end with a question. But, usually, I catch it after it's slipped. It irritates the holy crap out of me when I hear it. Even famous people and commentators have given in to this national obsession with speaking like this.

"You know," Big Black Guy says, "they really can't keep us here. We can leave if we want to. No tornado police comin' to get us if we leave." He chuckles and winks at no one in particular.

"But I think we should stay here where it's safe," Old Woman says.

We don't respond. We all just have that resigned-to-what-it-is look on our faces. So, I guess, here we'll stay. For some reason I think we all kind of *want* to stay. But that might just be my own weirdo thoughts.

The door opens again, and four more people come in to join us. They glance around for their sofa spots and all go in opposite directions. None of them are here together. They don't know each other. There are ten of us now. The door opens again and in comes number eleven. He's on crutches and his right foot is in one of those monster-sized black walking boots. And following close behind is number twelve. All of our eyes jump to number twelve. He's carrying two backpacks and half-dragging a third. His clothing is wet and in a type of disarray that we don't usually see. He goes to stand in the corner but faces us. He's rocking, swaying from one foot to the other.

"Store manipulized me coming here with you guys. I stay here," Rocking Man says. "Awared me of storm."

We all glance at each other. It's a way to acknowledge and validate our assessment: Rocking Man is...not quite like the rest of us. And I'm wondering if we're all hoping, as I am, that he's not here for tires...that he isn't driving a car.

"Mom traveled me here and she travel me home to get me," Rocking Man says. "Getting red birds when all the sudden, bang, bang, bang. Took me here."

In the bunch is a woman I'd guess to be about thirty-eight. She's attractive but not in that movie star kind of way. But, still, you notice her. She tosses off a cape-like thing that she's wearing and that's when you notice *them*...boobs. They are very big and very round and she's wearing a very tight-fitting sweater to make sure everyone does exactly this—notice them. I see Old Man and Crutches eyes meet in that subtle way men communicate without having to speak and without embarrassing anyone, including themselves.

"I wonder how long they'll keep us here?" Boobs says, "I have a lot to do today."

We are all murmuring things like, "Yeah." But we don't have a real answer for her.

Young Clerk comes back into our room. He's pushing a cart that has two black pitchers on it. You don't ever have to ask what's in those pitchers. Everyone knows that these black pitchers contain coffee and the one with the orange part on the handle is decaf. We all know this. There are two stacks of Styrofoam cups on the cart and three separate Styrofoam cups. One cup will have sugar in it, and substitutes, one will have creamer in it, either packets or little tubs of the flavored stuff, and the third cup you can see has little red and white striped stirrers standing at attention. There is a plate of cookies on a black plastic tray. Young Clerk grabbed his favorite kinds of cookies, ripped their packages open, and dumped the cookies onto the plate in no special arranged fashion. I can tell. But that's okay. They are Oreos and some other kind of tan-colored brand with chocolate chips in them. But Young Clerk is nineteen. This is his first job. He's nervous because of that, and he's nervous because of the tornado warning. Though the cookies don't look pretty, they do look edible to say the least. Some are chipped and some are broken. But Young Clerk did a good job with the two dozen cookies, minus the four he chomped on the way to our room. We all look pleased that he did this for us.

I get up. I am the first one to pour myself a cup of coffee. It smells wonderful and rich and hot and all of the glorious things that coffee is. It's much needed. I take a sip. Young Clerk did a good job. I grab two broken cookies. You can tell which broken pieces belong to which cookie.

Old Woman gets up and makes her way to the coffee cart. It's a given that she will fix a cup for Old Man too. It's a given that she will grab two of the cookie pieces and grin as she announces to us, "The pieces have no calories." I can tell. She's humming as she pours and stirs. She's been through many tornado warnings.

"Here you go, dear," she says, as she hands a cup to Old Man. She hands him two Oreos. Then she pivots and returns to the cart with light, almost silly little-girl-steps. She reaches for the cookies. "The pieces have no calories," she says, just as I knew she would, and she casts off a coy, dimpled grin as she snatches two cookie pieces. It doesn't matter how old you get; dimples hold their specialness and no one ever ages beyond using them to their fullest.

I just now notice another young woman in jeans. Her head is angled downward to her cellphone. She appears to be nearly attached to it by some invisible cable as she is busy texting. She hasn't said a word, and she surely won't be picking up one of the boring magazines.

There are a few minutes of silence as we munch and sip. You can't hear any of Boobs' sips or munches. She's being very dainty. Old Man makes an audible slurp every time he takes a sip of his coffee. I think this is both a cultural thing and an age-related thing. Rocking Man is humming. But, it's no specific or recognizable melody. It's in tune though. He's munching about five cookies all at the same time. Big Black Guy holds his Styrofoam cup in his left hand with his pinkie extended up. I've only seen people do that when they have a cup with a handle. In truth, I guess I've really only seen people hold up their pinkie in movies, comedies, actually. Big Black Guy is serious. I guess in his case, whatever floats your boat. Part of me would like to tell him all about his irksome habits. The key jingling and the pinkie brought me to this decision. It irritates me but I don't know why. I'm not going to say anything though. It was just a nasty, fleeing thought. I could address Cellphone's rude habit, too, just because she's isolated herself and is in her own private world over there with that dumb phone and probably having more fun than we are.

"Looks like you might be getting a late start on your fishing," Old Man says to Big Black Guy.

"It's okay. Plannin' on stayin' a week this time. Plenty of time to get out on the lake."

Tattoos snorts her coffee along with a cookie, almost choking. She's trying to stifle a laugh and let it out all at the same time. (You cannot breathe cookies and you cannot breathe coffee).

"Excuse me?" Tattoos says, clearing her throat, "but every time I hear someone talk about fishing it reminds me of a story about my dad and I get caught off guard and can't stop myself from laughing?" she says, laughing and coughing. She pats her chest. "Excuse me? Sorry."

We are all looking at her, not sipping or munching, as we're wondering where she's going with this and if she's really choking to death. But we're hoping, also, to hear the story. We have nothing else to do. We have nothing better to do. Tattoos coughs again to clear the cookie pieces out of her throat, and she wipes her mouth. She flicks away a stray laughter tear from her eye.

"My dad?" She begins but starts laughing again and chokes again. "Oh, sorry?" she says, "My dad was in Florida with a friend of his and the two of them decided that they were going to go out shrimping…fishing for shrimp? So, they rented a little boat and went out on the ocean? Neither of them had ever been out on the ocean. It was a picture-perfect sun shiny day, of course, I mean, it's Florida?

They had coffee with them and some sandwiches packed in a lunch box that my mom made for them? They had two big pails in the boat that they planned to put all of their shrimp in? I guess you dip nets or something into the water and scoop up shrimp. The friend was dipping for the shrimp, and my dad was steering and managing the boat until they found a spot to stop? Now they were both scooping up shrimp, and the pails were behind them? They were catching shrimp, and my dad told me that they'd whoop and holler when either of them scooped up two or three? They'd reach behind them and dump their shrimp into one of the pails and then return to scooping again? After about fifteen minutes, or so, his friend asked my dad, 'How many do we have?' My dad said he looked into the bucket, 'Six?' he told him. They kept scooping up a few shrimps here and there. 'How many do we have now?' My dad counted? 'Seven,' A few minutes later he asked again? 'Three? Next time it was eight? The next time my dad checked it was four? My dad said they were so happy catching shrimp that they were laughing like school boys. 'How many now?' After an hour. 'Sixteen.' The next check there were twelve?

"They stayed out on the ocean for a couple hours? 'We should probably get back now,' my dad decided, thinking that their wives would be worrying?

"His friend asks one last time, 'how many shrimps do we have to take back?' My dad said that he looked in the pail? 'Well, how many?' 'Two,' my dad said. 'That can't be. We've been out here for hours and we caught way more than that?' They both look into the pail. True. There were just two shrimp? At that moment those last two shrimp leaped right out of the pail and went back into the sea?"

We all bust out laughing. Gales of laughter. Laughter the size of ocean waves.

"Yeah," Big Black Guy says, "you gotta cover 'em."

"We had so many laughs about this in my family we call it The Shrimping Story?" Tattoos says. "Those guys took their ladies out for a shrimp dinner that night, but about all they did was laugh?"

"Oh, that's funny," Old Woman says, "but shrimp taste so good. At least they had fun trying. You never know 'til you try something. What amazes me is that we eat them at all…shrimp. Just think about that someone…that one person how many centuries ago. Someone had to be the first one to pick up that cold, scaled, multi-legged…thing… and decide, 'I'm going to eat this' and then did."

We all chuckle again.

"Ain't that the truth," Big Black Guy says. "I guess we chalk that up to human nature. And hunger."

And now it's quiet once more. We have resumed just sitting and staring…at not much of anything.

The overhead lights in The Waiting-Room flicker. But it's just a breath of a flicker. The building is huge and dense enough that we cannot hear thunder and there are no windows to see if it's raining and lightning. Surely, all of that is happening out there.

"I have a fish story too," one of the men says. "Your shrimp tale reminds me."

Nothing else to do. None of us has anything else we *can* do. Fish stories are making the time go by.

"It's not a fish story as much as it is, like, a fish…tradition," he says. "My folks are Scandinavian. So, we have, like, a yearly tradition on Christmas Eve that involves fish…a certain fish. Have you ever heard of lutefisk?"

The man glances at each of our faces in anticipation that at least one of us knows about this fish. Whether we do, or not, we aren't saying. Funny how no one wants to admit and no one ever wants to volunteer. It reminds me of being at a conference for work and the speaker asks for a volunteer. No one raises their hand because we don't know what we're getting into, we don't know what we're going to be asked to do or what might happen to us. I think we're most concerned about how everyone else in the room will perceive us if we do volunteer, and, heaven forbid, fail. We don't want to isolate ourselves or become too distant from the rest of the herd of turkeys.

So, here we sit. We are all smiling though, as we are waiting to hear another story about fish.

"Lutefisk is, like, a white-meat fish. Well, actually it's more transparent. Anyways there is this process that you go through to correctly prepare it for eating. Like, it takes several days of soaking it in a brine of some sort. My dad was, like, in charge of the lutefisk preparation but my mom cooked it when it was ready. Anyways, my dad had, like, some special store where he bought our lutefisk. He'd bring it home and it was all this, like, top-secret mission he was on. He'd take it down into the basement and it was, like, no one ever knew what he did down there with the fish. It was, like, his secret, but I do think it had something to do with soaking it in a special brine, a special recipe for about three days. Anyways, on Christmas Eve day my dad would bring the fish up to the kitchen and my mom would begin, like, preparing the Christmas Eve meal. Every Christmas Eve we would alternate having Christmas Eve at our parents' house or at my brother's home. But my dad still, like, bought and prepared the lutefisk, and we'd take it to my brother's house with us. We did it every year. Lutefisk doesn't take long to cook. You just slide it into a pot and, like, boil the snot out of it for, like, just a few minutes, I think, and then it's done. You, like, try to lift it out in one-nice-piece but there is no one-nice-piece with lutefisk. It, sort of, like, falls apart in the pot and you scoop out the pieces with a big spoon. My mom, or my sister-in-law then put it on a white platter. I have no idea why the platters were white. I think they were, like, just ours and that's what we had.

"Anyways, then you have this white fish on a white platter and you have baked potatoes that are also white, on the inside, and there is, like, this white-cream gravy that you put on the fish and your potato. We have crescent rolls…also what you'd call mostly white. Just think of all that white food sitting on your plate, like, staring up at you. The white gravy is needed because the fish has no flavor or texture of its own to it. It's basically, like, transparent and slimy. It falls apart, and you don't even have to, like, chew it at all. Just, like, slides down your throat. It even slides all around on your plate when you try to get a piece on your fork. You gotta run it up against a piece of potato or crescent roll to, like, block it in and get it on your fork. Lutefisk is the consistency, and look of…fish-flavored Jell-O. See-through, just like Jell-O is. But it's the gravy that has quite a few bits of, like, black pepper pieces in it that gives it anything like flavor. We might have some green beans or, like, some other green vegetable with it but I can never remember what it was. I just remember the fish-flavored Jell-O and all of that white meal. Anyways, year-after-year we did this," Lutefisk says shaking his head and smiling.

"I've read a few things about lutefisk but I've never met anyone who's actually eaten it or has used that tradition," Boobs says. "So does your dad or your brother do the lutefisk this coming Christmas Eve?"

"Neither," Lutefisk says. His smile trickles down his face and fades to gone. "When my dad passed away, like, a few years ago he took the tradition with him. We've never done it since his last Christmas."

The room is quiet and still, as we're all thinking, as I am, that they must have loved their dad so much that they just couldn't bear to have the special traditional meal without him and that only *he* knew how to do this. I can tell.

"We didn't stop having it because my dad died," Lutefisk says. "We stopped...because...we never even, like, discussed it because there was no need. I think we all knew that we did this year-after-year just because it was, like, important to our dad. But if you want to know the truth," Lutefisk says, squishing his lips together to rein in a laugh. "We have never said, but some things you just don't have to, like, say. We *hated* it and we don't miss it. I miss my dad, but I think I would have liked the tradition more if it involved...like, omelets."

At that, we all burst into laughter again. Lutefisk is funny. He knows it. He's talked about lutefisk many times before and it always gets a good laugh.

"I've heard about the fish," Old Man says, "but I've never had the honor of trying it."

"You're, like, not missing much," Lutefisk says.

"I've heard of it too," Old Woman says, "but you tell the story so well. I guess what's important is that tradition can keep us going as a family. Maybe you will start it up again one day."

Lutefisk shakes his head with precision. "Not gonna happen," he says. "Like, not ever."

Old Woman gets up and takes the coffee pot around to each of us. She tops off the cups for those who want another splash. Cellphone doesn't look up from her gadget. So, Old Woman skips over her. She returns to sit beside Old Man.

"I don't have another fish story," Tattoos says, "but I do have a dad story and I really would just like to tell someone?"

Everyone nods. Bobbleheads at work again.

"Sure, sweetie. Go ahead," Old Man says, tenderly, and picking up on the change in her tone. I've noticed that old people are able to pick up such subtleties as a change in tone. Not me. I've tried. But I'm not that old yet.

I just came from Florida visiting my folks? My dad is a retired fireman? Most amazing man I've ever known? Most amazing man I will *ever* know? He can do everything? Taught me to ride my bike? He taught me how to ride a motorcycle? Taught me how to change the oil in any car? He's the most solid man. He's always been the one I turn to and the one I look up to and rely on to give me the truth about anything? He's always been the greatest driver? He never got stuck and he could get anybody's car unstuck from snow or mud? He's never had a traffic accident in his life? You could always count on my dad getting our family safely wherever we had to go? He has always been *the* driver whether it was taking us to and from school or out to the Grand Canyon and all over for vacations? He never expected anyone else to drive. He did it all? And everybody wanted him to drive. It was just so…the-way-it's-supposed-to-be when he drove? You felt so safe? Even when I had my friends go places with us, their parents would always ask, 'your dad's driving, right?' This is hard to explain," Tattoos says. She sucks in a long, heavy breath and then exhales with a quick puff. "I don't know why I'm telling you all this…"

"Please, keep going," Boobs says, "we *have* to hear."

Tattoos clears her throat, as we all do before saying something personal, offensive, or not true. She thinks something's stuck there but nothing is. She coughs. She's going to tell us the personal type of story.

"Excuse me," she says, "must be a cookie piece?" She coughs again.

"Yeah," someone says, "those cookie pieces will get you every time." But we're not paying attention to who said this. We want to hear the story.

"I'll try to explain?" Tattoos says, "I just hope this makes sense to you? Okay. Like I said, I just came back from Florida. I flew into St. Pete's at night? They were waiting for me, all happy and smiling? They had tears in their eyes, and I just flew into their arms? I haven't seen them in a year? That's too long, ya know, to see your parents? But they know I can't always afford to make the trip and when dad retired and they moved to Florida? they didn't plan to come back home? I'd have to go see them? We got my bags, and my dad wheeled one bag, and I carried the smaller one? I could tell it was about eighty-degrees and it felt wonderful? I couldn't wait to smell the warmth of Florida and the flowers and the orange blossoms? When we got to their car, I put my hand on the backseat door handle? 'How about you drive?' my dad said. I didn't know what to say? I didn't know what to do? My mom quietly got in the car in the front seat and my dad climbed into the *back* seat? I just stood there for a few seconds trying to make sense of this? But then it hit me like a ton of bricks: My dad no longer had the confidence to drive. I thought maybe only at night? I was so shocked?"

Tattoos shakes her head slowly as she wriggles her fingers around together. But she's not twiddling her thumbs. She's just wriggling all of her fingers. If she looks up at any of us, or if I say anything, her tears will flood the room.

"Anyway," Tattoos says. "I'm glad it was night because I had a hard time not crying at the change in my dad? I never once dreamed that this would ever happen. Not to *my* dad, the rock of ages? *My* rock of ages?"

What are you going to say? Who's going to say something first? Tattoos finally lifts her head up. She looks at each of us. She has a shortened version of a smile on her face. She went to Florida as daddy's good little girl, and in that moment that he asked her to take the wheel, she instantly became a forever adult, complete with her own assignment of mortality.

Old Man is the first to speak. "That's beautiful," he says almost in a whisper. "If your father could hear you talk about him in such a wonderful manner as you have, he'd be so proud of you. And, he'd know that he really reached you and taught you when you were growing up and under his care. Not every daughter can realize the significance of that experience. So many young people would have just said, 'yeah, sure, Pop' and taken the wheel without a thought about why it happened."

"And," Old Woman says, "here is something for you to remember. Though you're all grown up now and have a life all your own… you will always be his baby girl. Even though he's handed the steering wheel over to you, you will always be his baby. Even if you become the President of the United States, you will still be his baby girl."

Tattoos nods and smiles. "I think you're right?" she says. "I have so many good memories of my dad and my mom. It's just hard to think of them aging? Hard to see how much that changes a person? The best memory I have is the one night I came home early from work early because there was a snow storm and I wanted to get home? I was working at a women's shelter sorting clothing and stuff that people donated? Anyway, I came home about ten that night. The lights were on in the house but I couldn't find anyone? I was a little bit worried but then I heard music? I went to the back door and peeked outside into the yard? My mom and dad were out there? They had brought out their ancient record player and put it on the picnic table? My dad had hooked it to one of those orange outdoor extension cords? They had two lit candles on the picnic table, and there was a bottle of wine with two glasses? The porch light was on, too, so I could see all of this, but just barely? Huge flakes of snow were coming down and sticking to their knit caps and on their shoulders? They were up to their knees in the fresh snow? Their bodies were pressed up tight against each other and they were dancing? Dancing in the snow. My mom was looking right up into my dad's eyes as he held her, and she'd toss her head back every minute or so and giggle as he guided her along. And he was grinning, too, as he was talking to her? Dancing, swaying so perfectly as one out there in the snow. It was cold? I could see their breaths? I just went up to my room and let them be? They never knew I came home early that night," Tattoos says. "Dancing in the snow? I've never shared that with anyone."

Now *I* want to dance in the snow. We *all* want to dance in the snow. We all want to try it. Snow is generally a wicked glob of stuff to deal with. It's more than an inconvenience. I hate it. Now I want to try to dance in it.

"You're a special young lady," Old Man says. "Sometimes I worry about the younger generations. I worry about our young people. I worry about kids and what it's going to be like for them…what it's going to be like with them when it's their turn to take over. But you have that certain feel for life that seems lacking in so many. You, young lady… you understand it. You understand it now. You understand life and the meanings. You understand the significance that goes along with our experiences as we make our way through life. Thank you for sharing about your parents because you have sweetly educated me, *reminded* me, to have faith in young people."

I don't even have to look to know that we all have misty eyes. I have mist in my eyes. But none of us wants anyone else to see these eyeballs of ours. Powerful sentences. A strong bridge erected right in front of all of these misty eyes. For us. This is all like watching a good drama on TV.

Old Woman appropriately gets up and pours herself another cup of coffee and she motions with it to Old Man. He shakes his head. He's had enough but she already knew that. Old Woman then holds the pot out in front of her to the rest of us without saying anything. I lift my cup. She fills it and then fills for Tattoos. She motions to Rocking Man. "I'll fix a cup for you," she says. "Would you like a cup of coffee?"

"Noper. Not me," Rocking Man says. "Cookies. Like my cookies."

Old Woman sits back down a little closer to Old Man.

"You know," Crutches says, "the aging thing reminds me of my dogs. They really aren't much different than we are…dogs. I used to have a super sweet border collie-cross dog. Found her running the streets. Named her Lexie. She fit in well with my older dog, Stanley, a boxer-cross. I'd take them both out walking every day. They always walked side-by-side as if they'd been trained to do that. But they weren't trained to do that. They just decided to pace themselves and stay side-by-side out in front of me on their leashes. They'd prance along so happy. After a few years, Stanley started slowing down. His face turned mostly white and he couldn't prance anymore. Stanley was really aging a lot more, it seemed, every day. You know, once a dog starts to age, it all happens so fast. Lexie was still full of herself and full of life. Stanley got to the point where he'd be walking behind us, me in the middle, and Lexie out front. I would think, and think *to* Lexie, that someday she'd be able to go as fast as she wanted again because it would just be me and her. Then one day Stanley passed on. He died right in my kitchen. Man, that was tough," Crutches says.

I think I hear a slight tremble in his words. He continues.

"So then, Lexie and me had the walks to ourselves and she could once again prance ahead of me and at the pace she chose. We had a few years of just the two of us. Then one day another young dog came along that needed a home. Stuart is just a brown, no-idea-what-he-is mutt. He's goofy and happy every minute of the day and full of that energy that puppies and young dogs have. So, all three of us could go on our daily walks. Then the day comes along when Lexie is the one walking slowly behind us, and Stuart is out front, and I'm thinking the same thing, that one day it will be just the two of us, just me and Stuart, and he will be able to go the speed he wants again. Sure enough, I lost Lexie, too. Now it's just me and goofy Stuart."

Crutches looks down and then looks up and off to the right as if there should be something there for him to see. But, it's just the corner of the room.

"So, that's my dog story," he says. "Somehow it just ties in with this whole age thing and that no matter who we are we're just passing through. Dogs get replaced. We're sure to be replaced too. I don't know…I just wanted to tell you. Just seems to fit."

Strange how this works. I guess we can chalk that up to human nature once again. When someone tells a poignant story, such as Tattoos did, it doesn't matter if it's funny or sad or powerful, we all want to come up with something that also has an effect on others. We want that approval from others for ourselves. I don't think of it as competition as much as I think we have a need for appreciation, for validation, and we want a chance to feel included.

Rocking Man is humming. He's smiling. He's smiling more at the center of the room than at any one of us. I wonder what makes him smile? What prompts him to rock?

"I have question," a man begins. He hasn't spoken before. He has an accent. He's not Black but he has a darker skin color. He could be a terrorist. I can tell. If we were to ask him if he's a terrorist, of course, he's going to say "no" and tell us that he's not a terrorist. Why would any terrorist admit that? He's looking at Old Man and Old Woman.

"How long been married?" Accent asks.

Old Man and Old Woman both throw their heads back and laugh probably the biggest guffaw I've ever heard. We all start to laugh at what we guess to be some type of inside joke or story. I have a moment of feeling left out and I'm sure everyone else feels this for some fleeting seconds because we aren't on the inside of this story. Only Old Man and Old Woman have the inside scoop.

"We're..." Old Man says, trying to block another laugh, "we're on our honeymoon," he says.

Old Man and Old Woman are laughing now and leaning into each other so that their shoulders would be cramped if they didn't love it. Old Man winks at Old Woman.

"Oh, you silly thing," she says, looking into his eyes and giving him a soft whack on the shoulder.

The rest of us are smiling but our mouths are open. Shocked. Happy shocked.

"You joke," Accent says.

"No," Old Man says. We got married last week." He says with a half-giggle, "We eloped. We got married at a chapel in Vegas. We just took off and did it."

"Amazing. When you meet?"

"It's quite a story," Old Man says.

The rest of us probably have to hear the whole thing for it to make sense. I guess I need to hear it. I *want* to hear this story.

"It all started about seventy-six years ago," Old Man says. "We were next-door neighbors. Just little kids. We were both six when she and her family moved into the house across my yard."

"My first memory of this fella," Old Woman says, "was when I saw him running around his back yard, dashing left and right, stopping and starting, stopping and starting. He had his shoulders all scrunched up to his ears and that's how he was running. Seeing him run like that scared me. I thought something was horribly wrong with him. I even asked my mother what was wrong with that little boy. My mother looked out the window. But, by that time, this flaming red-headed streak had sat under a tree. Then the next day, there he was out there again running and dashing all over the yard all hunched up. I marched over there and yelled at him to stop. 'What are you doing?' I asked. 'I'm a football player,' he said, 'See? I have a football.' And off he went again. I hadn't noticed the football until he showed it to me. All I had been interested in was his deformity. I told my mother that he had a football and that he said he's a football player.

"My mother looked out the window. He was out there, zooming all around his yard again with his football. My mother started laughing. She knew instantly what the wild red-headed creature was doing. He had no idea that football players actually wore shoulder pads. All he knew is that they were running around with their shoulders up to their ears so that's what he did. He pushed his shoulders up as high as he could to look just like the real players."

"I didn't know they used shoulder pads for about another year, or two," Old Man says, laughing.

"There were no other little girls or little boys nearby so we started spending our time together," Old Man says. "We had no one else."

"He'd insist on me catching and tossing that football," Old Woman says, "and I didn't like it."

"You made me have tea parties with your dolls," Old man says, "I had to get something out of it."

"But I actually liked playing with the football more than the tea parties," Old Woman says as she casts us a wink and flashes those dimples.

"We spent every spring and summer, every fall and winter, playing. We were always together," Old Man says. "One day I told her that we were boyfriend and girlfriend and she agreed. But we didn't know what that meant other than you say you have a boyfriend or a girlfriend because all of the other kids at school were saying that."

"Remember the time we got stuck on the monkey bars?" Old Woman says.

"I do," Old Man says. "You see, we both climbed up onto the monkey bars, the kind you climb up like a ladder, and on top of that is what looks like another ladder on top connecting the other two sets of rungs. When you are on top you grasp the bars on each side and pull along and then scoot your butt and legs over each rung until you get to the other end, turn around and then climb down. Well, on that day, we each climbed a ladder on opposite ends and started the scooting along until we were face-to-face. I'll never forget the look on her face…"

"Or on your face…"

"Because we both had no clue what to do then or how to get back down. She kept telling me to turn around and I kept telling her to turn around but neither of us knew how to do that up there on top of the monkey bars smackdab in the middle. Before that time, we'd always started climbing up the ladder from the same end and followed each other. But on that day, we'd each climbed up on the opposite ends and then gone forward until we met in the middle of the thing and we'd never had to turn around up on top before. The bell went off, and everyone ran back into the school. There we sat. Stuck. Our teacher came out. We knew by the speed she was coming, and by the look on her face, that she wasn't very happy with us. 'You get down from there,' she says. I said we can't. We don't know how. 'You got up there, now you just turn your little selves around and climb down,' she said. Then we both started to cry, and not because we were stuck, but because we were afraid of her. We knew there was a paddling in the plans for us. Our teacher stood under the bars flailing her arms all around trying to grab one of our legs. We spun our legs around like propellers to avoid her. We were even more scared because we thought she'd pull us to the ground and that would be the end our lives. So, we kept swinging our legs all over so she couldn't grab us, and we tightly gripped the bars with our hands. They had to call the fire department to get us down. We were declared heroes from that point on. We were the school celebrities for years. But we never went back up on the monkey bars. I still don't think I'd know how to turn around up there and head back the way I'd come."

"Remember when I got stuck in the mud?" Old Woman chimes in, smiling up at her husband." He nods and grins.

"We'd been out playing for recess and there was a huge amount of mud where the field was," Old Woman says. "Of course, I went out into the mud just like everyone else did, like the bigger kids did. The bell rang. Once again, our teacher, same teacher, came swooping out there like a hawk ready to dive for prey. 'You get out of the mud right now, missy,' she said. I told her I couldn't because I was stuck. I truly couldn't move either foot. My boots were stuck almost to their tops.

She didn't believe me. She didn't believe me then because she always believed that I could've gotten down from the monkey bars. So, naturally, I was lying about the mud too. The teacher grabbed my arm and pulled me to her. She pulled me clean out of my boots. I came flying towards her and landed standing up in front of her on the paved parking lot in my new Christmas socks. And there were my boots, stuck in the mud right where I'd been pulled out of them. She did fetch my boots out of the mud. She never said anything. She knew then that I was telling the truth. I think from that point on, she realized that me and this guy here would naturally attract trouble. So, she left us alone. And, it was this guy who dared me to go out into the mud with the bigger kids in the first place. He dared me to go out there. He was, and still is, a scoundrel."

"Oh, don't you believe it," Old Man says.

"Well you *are* and you know it," Old Woman says.

"Grade school passed," Old Man says, "and then came junior high school. We were in some of the same classes. I carried her books to classes for her and she'd bring me a sandwich from home or brownies that she said she made herself, but I know now that she didn't make them because she didn't know how to bake or cook. No way she made those brownies."

Old Woman tosses her head and winks at Old Man. She laughs and looks at us. "It's true," she says, "but I got better at it."

"Anyway," Old Man says, "she was growing up and becoming beautiful. Too beautiful for her own good. Of course, by that time I was noticing much more than her agility, or lack of agility, on the monkey bars. I remember the day I was sitting in 9th grade math class. She was two desks in front of me and to my right and I saw her as if there was no one else in the room at that moment, even though the classroom was full. I saw her in slow motion, like in the movies, as she tossed her golden-brown hair, all in curls, over her shoulder. Perfect teeth, perfect lips, perfect face in every way. I could just see her budding figure pressing against her cardigan, if you get what I mean, as she partially turned to face two other boys. She tossed her pretty hair over her shoulder. She *knew* what she was doing. She *knew* that as she sat there laughing and flashing her smile that she had them under her spell. We were fourteen, fifteen, and that's when you start awakening in earnest. You wake up from being a little kid and begin crossing over into awareness of your sexuality and the adult wanting to emerge. I will never forget that day when I realized that she was more than my little childhood buddy. I felt it in my body for the first time. Part of me enjoyed seeing her mesmerize the other boys because I knew she was *mine*. We were boyfriend and girlfriend, right? But part of me felt that strong emotion of jealousy percolating.

"When we started high school, on the first day, I caught up with her in the hallway. She was walking with two of her girlfriends. As I approached her, I saw her as the most beautiful girl I'd ever seen in my life. She'd perfected swaying her hips just enough that boys noticed, and she'd perfected that hair toss. Tiny waist. Nice legs. She had it all. And…she knew it. The boys fell at her feet like a human carpet in front of her. I fell in love with her on that day. Not puppy love on that day, real love. We only had one class together from then on for that year and then never again. I carried her books that day for the last time. Then a distance developed between us. Now I can look back and I'm sure we both felt it at the time but had no way of knowing what it was. Even though we were growing up, and apart, we were always there for each other."

"Like when my father died," Old Woman says. "It was my first time with death. I was sixteen. My father died unexpectedly of a heart attack right when he was sitting at the breakfast table in front of me and my mother. So sudden. I ran out the door and flew into his house, and he put his arms around me and held me as I cried so hard. I couldn't breathe because I was so scared. He came to the funeral and sat right next to me and held my hand, so gently, petting it. It seems like it takes a lifetime to get over the loss of your papa."

Old Woman looks at each of us and we appropriately nod, solidifying her statement.

"But you do go on," Old Woman says. "This guy was the first person I told that I wanted to become a nurse. I'll never forget that day. He hugged me and when I faced him, he leaned very close to me and then he kissed me on the lips. It was my first kiss ever and I just wanted to explode with joy. But I couldn't. I couldn't let myself. I was afraid. I refused to allow myself to openly enjoy it and to tell him anything. We just stood there then and looked at each other not knowing what to do or what to say. He was there for me, always, as my best friend. He always just listened, and hugged me, no matter what I had to tell him We always sat on the porch swing. That's all that mattered. It just mattered that I got to tell someone and that he listened and hugged me. We sat on that swing and talked about everything. He was there for me when I wanted to surprise my mother and wallpaper the den. We did it together. We made a great mess, but we sure had fun laughing and getting goo all over the place. But the wallpaper was good, though a little crooked in spots, and my mother was so happy, so surprised, that we had done this all for her.

"He was playing football in high school. I went to the games but I always went with another boy to watch and be a part of all of the high school events. Every now and then I'd see him look up into the stands to find me and when our eyes met, I'd nod and he'd get this huge, silly grin on his face. The boy I was with would always see it and look more than a little miffed. I never knew that I was in love with him then. I was afraid of these strong and new emotions."

"She could have any boy she wanted," Old Man says. "She was the most popular girl in school and she'd drifted up higher than me and out of my reach. I knew that. But I knew even then that I was so completely in love with her I almost couldn't stand it."

"But," Old Woman says, "you never said it. You never told me then."

Old Man nods, eyes closed. "You never let on either."

"She was there for me too. I played football in school but I wasn't good enough. I wasn't tall enough, not big enough, and I didn't stand out to get a scholarship. I knew, then, that I'd never become pro. She was there for me and listened and got teary-eyed with me when I told her that my folks said I have to think of something else. They didn't have money to send me to college and without a scholarship it was out of the question. The only option for me was the Army. So, I signed up right out of high school. For a while, we kept in touch. We never said, but we always knew we were there for each other. We signed our letters with love but we both hid the real meaning of that word. My parents were killed in a car accident, and I came home to bury them. We got together then, but of course with the stress of the loss and funerals, it wasn't a happy time."

"When he was ready to leave again," Old Woman says, "I told him that I was getting married. The look on his face was such devastation. I'd never seen that on anyone. I've never seen anyone look so destroyed…not once in my life…not before and I've never seen a look like that since. I thought maybe it was a mistake for me to get married. But we'd never said. We'd never once talked about a forever life *together*. Not once did we even speak of marriage, for us, together. So,

I got married. My marriage lasted only one year and my new husband took off with my best friend. We divorced. I got married again and that one lasted only eight months. Then I got married again and had twin daughters. That marriage came to an end also."

Now, we are all sitting on the edge of our sofa spots, falling into the story. Of course, we want to know how many times Old Woman has been married.

"She's been married five times," Old Man says. "And just in case you're wondering, I'm number six."

"Oh, you. You didn't have to tell them *that*," Old Woman says. But she laughs and says, "It's true. I just never got it right. Until now. I spent my whole life searching for what I thought every time was the right thing, and I never found it. I did become a nurse and I stayed right in our home town. I never left. I was busy raising my two girls and then I lost everything when our home burned to the ground. We got out but I lost everything. When people say those are just material things you lose…well…that's not really accurate and it's not compassionate because it's the only proof of your existence that you'll ever have. It's the only proof of the life you lived before the fire. That's what you truly lose. Those things *do* matter and it's unkind to tell someone that they don't matter or for you to tell yourself that they don't matter. You lose all *proof* that you'd been alive and that you had a life. I did leave town then. I just wanted to leave and start new somewhere else. So, my girls and I left and moved over a hundred miles away. I got a job at another hospital, and I was able to buy a nice little house eventually. My girls grew up. It was funny how they'd always laugh at me whenever there was a football game on television or a football story in the news showed some famous football player because I would giggle. They'd ask me what was so funny. But I never told them. It was a private, special memory just for me. And, then as the years went on, they stopped asking.

39

They accepted, and then ignored, that whenever I saw football players it would make me giggle. I never told them. You see, I saw *this* fellow in my memories, that little boy running all around with his shoulders all pushed up to his ears. Time went on. One of my girls got married and moved to Fort Wayne with her husband who is a newspaper editor. The other one hasn't married and prefers the single life. She paints rooms for people and does some interior design work though she's never been to school for it. She's doing okay. One day, when I realized they were both out of the house and on their own, I remember looking in the mirror and trying to remember what I had looked like as a young woman. My school yearbooks and all photos of me had been lost in the fire. The only memory of me was the one looking back at me in the mirror. I'd taken up dying my gray hair. I no longer remembered what my natural-color hair looked like. There were wrinkles. Did I always have them? I guessed not, but I had nothing to compare it to. At times, I thought about this guy," she says, caressing Old Man's cheek with the back of her hand. "Where is he? What's he doing? Who did he marry? Does he have kids? Does he still have that fiery red hair?"

"And for me," Old Man says, "I lost her. Nowadays life is so fast and with computers and social media there are so many ways to find people. You can find anyone. But back then...I just lost her. I moved up the ranks in the Army. I was overseas a lot. I was in the jungle. I fought, I trained and I did just about everything for this country you can think of. I did marry. What else was I supposed to do? I tried to find this girl but I never got a response from her. I didn't know her last name. I didn't know where she was. I went home once after I couldn't reach her, and a new family lived in my childhood home. It was all different. The last house I knew she had lived in was gone. There was a convenience store in its place. I didn't know what happened, and I didn't really want to know what had happened. I never went to a school reunion. I just didn't go. I was busy in the Army."

"I don't know why," Old Woman says, "but I never went to a reunion either. There'd been too many husbands, I think. I guess it was, maybe, a final coming of age type of thing, maybe more of a pride thing, embarrassed maybe, that I hadn't done as well as the other girls."

Old Woman appears sort of stuck before she speaks again. Just a few seconds pass but it almost seems like she can't make the words come out of her mouth

"I'm wondering, dear," she says, "if you should tell them that you played football?"

Didn't we just hear about football?

"Oh," Old Man says, "I think you did a great job when you told them all about that."

"Okay," Old Woman says. "So, they know you played football?"

"Yes, dearest," Old Man says. He squeezes her hand.

"Anyway," Old Man says, "I married a nice woman but during our vows I was thinking of this one," he says as he pushes his shoulder tighter against Old Woman's shoulder. "I had a decent marriage. We had a daughter and two sons. But I lost my wife when she was only sixty. Stroke. That's way too young to go. Losing my wife was hard on everyone. It was hard on me and the kids. We all know that we're going to lose loved ones, but it doesn't make it any easier knowing that, and it sure doesn't make it any easier when it happens. I loved my wife though I don't think I was *in* love with her. I'd only felt that kind of love once in my life and that was that day it hit me in school. That's when I knew what love is. But I guess I was too young, or too proud, to know, or to do anything with it. I didn't know what it was when it hit me.

"I never considered myself a religious man. But one day I prayed and asked God if He really was there, and if He really cared, to please bring my girl back into my life. I told Him I was an old man now and time was running out.

"Weeks and years marched on, and I got even older. Then one day, not too long ago, a golf buddy of mine wanted me to take him to the Emergency Room just to be checked out because he had a catch when he tried to take a breath. So, we went. I waited out in the lobby. Something told me to look down the hall to my left and the moment I saw the woman walking toward me…I knew. It was her. I stood up. She stopped walking. She knew. We both knew. I never took my eyes off her, and we started walking to each other a little faster with each step. There was no hesitation, not even a slight hesitation, as she flew into my arms just like old times when we were kids and I wrapped her as tight as I could. Oh, did we have some tears. We never said anything for the longest time. It felt like hours went by. Hours of missed hugs. Hours of closeness. Just that once in a lifetime hug. A forever-hug. And we cried together. We were both shaking, remember that, dear one?"

Old Woman nods and smiles sweetly and leans closer into her man. "I cried, too, didn't I?"

"Yes, my love. We both did," Old Man says.

"Okay," Old Woman says.

"After our sniffling stopped," Old Man says, "we dabbed each other with tissue that she pulled from her smock pocket, and then we sat down on a hospital lobby bench at talked. She had retired as a nurse from that hospital and was doing volunteer work taking patients and family where they needed to go, answering questions, and just being a source of help and comfort.

"We held hands and we walked outside into a cool breeze. We sat at a table in the yard of the hospital. I knew time was ticking away for both of us. So, I cut right to it and asked her to marry me. She said yes as tears ran down her face."

"Yours too," Old Woman says.

"Yes, I did cry," Old Man says, "I bawled. I'm so happy that I finally have this girl. She's every bit as beautiful as she was when I first noticed her beauty. But I grew up knowing she was beautiful. Beautiful inside and out. She's always been my one and only best friend. Love happens, and it's real. And dreams and prayers do come true no matter how old you happen to be. It can happen any time."

"Wow," Lutefisk says on a breath. "Wow. Like, major wow."

"Quite a story," Boobs says. "Very inspiring…to think that you guys got together after all these years."

"Yes," Old Woman says, "this is who I was supposed to be with all along. I just never knew it. No, that's not correct. I never *admitted* it. I think maybe because we grew up, we grew into each other and into the relationship, the friendship, as it was, and I think there was this unspoken understanding that we'd always be together. But we never said it when we were old enough, but still young enough, to say it. Maybe we just got used to each other always being there."

"But just think if you had gotten married back then, you wouldn't have the kids and families you have now," Big Black Guy says.

"Yes," Old Woman says, "but if we had gotten married back then, the children we have now would have never been in existence. We would have never known them. So, it's not like if we had gotten married then we would have deleted our children. They would have never been in the running. We'd have had different children. But things do have a way of still working out the way they are supposed to. People sometimes get in the way of the plans, but God has a way of *still* getting His way."

"And you know," Old Man says, "it doesn't matter how much time we have left together. All that matters now is today. And today we are having so much fun, and we are so much in love."

"And I get to baby him and wait on him and fuss over him and make him all of his favorite foods," Old Woman says.

"She can bake her own brownies now. From scratch. She's a great cook. Now," Old Man says. "She learned over the years, and she bakes the best brownies. And I bring her coffee every morning while she's still in bed,"

"He does," Old Woman says.

"And I bring her roses. Sometimes I bring them every day."

"He does," Old Woman says.

"It's an incredible story?" Tattoos says. "I would love to have a real love story like that?"

"Me too," Boobs says.

"We *all* like story as that one," Accent says.

"They still happen," Old Man says. "Just don't give up. Don't rush into a replacement thing when you know you have reservations about doing it. Wait for the right one. And, probably the most important advice I can give you is to say it when you're supposed to say it. Don't let fear or pride clutter the way in front of you. Say what you need to say when you need to say it."

I guess I have to admit that I'm shocked. I was wrong. And I guess I have to admit that it kinda makes me feel really good to be shocked in this way. It actually makes me feel good to be wrong. Who would have thought they were on their honeymoon? I sure didn't expect to hear that. Their story kinda makes the news this morning fade away and it helps take the sting out of the bubble-wrap trauma.

So, now we sit again. No one has a story that can outshine that one. But we're hoping that one of us comes up with something to chat about so we don't go back to staring at our feet or, heaven forbid, shuffling through a magazine we have no interest in. But there are times when silence is okay. We only *feel* that we're supposed to be yacking every minute and that if we aren't something is wrong with us. I guess I feel the same way, but I can't think of anything to say. I'm glancing around the room. Everyone meets my eyes and smiles that kind of sheepish I-don't-know-what-to-do smile. How do you top *that* story?

Old Woman wipes a cookie crumb off her upper lip. "Should we tell them about us getting stuck on the monkey bars?"

I've grown fond of Old Woman since we've been together in The Waiting-Room and a sadness slices into me because she's forgotten that the story about the monkey bars was already told. I think I understand now. She shifts her body in a way that lets me know she is also aware that her memory fails her. But Old Man handles her forgetfulness with class.

"Oh, we might do that," Old Man says.

"Okay," Old Woman says. "It's a good story." Old Woman is smiling and she appears content again.

Then Old Woman looks at Tattoos. "I don't mean to pry," she says, "well maybe I do, but can I ask you something?"

"Sure?" Tattoos says.

"Why do you have so many tattoos? Why isn't one enough?"

Oh boy. Here we go.

"I love them?" Tattoos says. "Each one has a special meaning to me and you don't get them all at one time?"

Tattoos pauses before speaking again. She has a puzzled look on her face. She's wondering if this conversation has now launched into alien-speak. I think.

"Let me put it this way?" she says. "I see that you have gemstone earrings? They look like emeralds? You have your wedding rings, of course, on your left hand but you have, one, two…three, four other rings on your right hand and another one on your pinky? On the left hand you have two more rings? You are also wearing a gold ankle bracelet?"

Old Woman nods and smiles. She winks at Old Man. He's given her all of those baubles. I'm guessing.

"So?" Tattoos says, "why isn't one ring enough? They were probably all gifts, or, you bought them because they reminded you of someone or some memory? Maybe they were just pretty and you wanted them? My tattoos are the same for me? Jewelry? Expressions of me… expressions of memories or dreams and what's important to me?"

"But I can take my jewelry off if I don't want to wear any of it or if I just want to wear one piece," Old Woman says.

"Some things are meant to be for life?" Tattoos says. "I've chosen each time I've gotten a tat that I won't want to take it off? It's not *just* jewelry? It's art? You don't just take art off the wall and set it aside? I don't anyway."

"But might you regret having all of those tattoos when you turn eighty?"

"What if I don't live to be eighty?"

Old Woman blushes. Maybe because she's passed her eightieth birthday already by a few years. Maybe she's blushing because she realizes that she's not grasping something. Maybe she's blushing because she can no longer count the miles of distance between her and Tattoos. Age. The difference of culture and the distance of many miles between them. This can cause you to feel embarrassed.

"But when I die, I can leave these pieces to my daughters or to someone who I know would appreciate them. You will take the tattoos with you," Old Woman says.

"Oh, ha, ha, ha," Rocking Man sings to us. "No one want your stuff when croak. Think do. Don't. Nobody do. Gonna dump to garbage. Bye-bye stuff. Bye-bye you. Garbage time. Don't stumple on. Gone, gone. All gone. No more you. No more stuff."

We all screech to an emotional halt. I think we've all even stopped breathing. Rocking Man is still rocking and now he's humming and smiling but not to us. And we *are* stumped. Part of it is comical but that little scene seared into each of us down into somewhere we don't have a name for. I'm thinking of all those garage sales and estate sales that overtake yards in the summertime. There are boxes and crates of collectibles and books and photos that meant something to someone when he took the photo or when she started that collection of frog figurines. Maybe Rocking Man is right. No one wants *our* stuff. They want their own stuff.

Finally, Old Woman smiles. She knows she is supposed to be the first one to speak.

"I think it makes more sense to me now," she says. "We're all different in the things we like. So, thank you. I was a little afraid to ask. I've never asked anyone about tattoos, though I've wanted to. You explained it well. Maybe I should try it." Old Woman turns to Old Man, "What do you think? Think I should get a tattoo?"

"Whatever makes you happy, I will be happy," Old Man says.

Old Woman relaxes against the sofa. She's smiling and I just saw her wink at Tattoos. Something tells me that Old Woman just might get that tattoo.

And now I'm uncomfortable again. It might have been better if Old Woman hadn't said a word to start the tattoos conversation and to toss Rocking Man into action. But at least, now, we have an understanding of tattoos. I'm uncomfortable thinking about all of those garage sales and the countless collections of stuff that belonged to someone at some time when that person was alive.

So, what will happen to my stones? When I was a kid, I started collecting a stone from every state in the country. Most of them I picked up myself but some I asked friends to bring back for me. I have fifty stones and each one is in a little case with its state name written on the box. What will I do with them? Who will want them? It stings right now because Rocking Man forced me to realize that I am the only person on this planet who will ever want my stones. Now the next question pours into my thoughts. How much time do *I* have left? These thoughts can really add to your depression or kick it back in gear just when you thought it was gone.

"Well," Big Black Guy says, "we've heard about critters and fish and shrimp and love and tattoos. I think we're covering it pretty dog-gone well."

The Bobbleheads, once again, are dipping and rising in response. We are also, once again, out of time with each other. I might be the only one who notices that.

And then the door opens. It always seems like someone comes along who just rubs you the wrong way. They don't fit in. Sullen. I guess is what I would call a person like that is sullen. In blows this other woman into The Waiting-Room. She spins down onto a chair, secluded, and not on a spot on a sofa. She crosses her arms in front of her chest and stares at the floor. She's wearing a sort of blondish-hued, dark-streaked wig. You can tell that this is most definitely a wig. It doesn't match her complexion. But I guess it's her choice what she wants to put on her head.

"Hello," Old Woman says. "How is your day going? We are all stuck here in this room waiting out the warning and the storm. But we're having quite a bit of fun along with coffee and cookies."

"Good for you," Sullen says with a forced and fake-as-plastic smile. You can always tell when it's forced because only the lips move. But they, too, want to stick in place like the covering on that new DVD you just bought. The eyes and the rest of the face don't smile along. Sullen grabs a magazine without even choosing one. I know she just grabbed it to let Old Woman know that she doesn't want to chat with her.

"Happy birthday," Rocking Man says to Sullen.

Surprised. Taken aback, Sullen's eyes snap to Rocking Man. She snaps her words out too. "It's not my birthday. Sorry," she says and zooms her eyes back down to her magazine.

"Be someday. Happy birthday today for birthday when birthday day come. Like birthdays."

Sullen makes a slight smirk and a barely audible huffing sound. It's hard to tell if she's softening or if she thinks Rocking Man is ridiculous. Probably a little of both. I feel kind of bad for Rocking Man. He was just being in the moment, just as he always is. He was just trying to be nice in a way that only he understands. He was just being Rocking Man and he is part of our group in The Waiting-Room. I feel a closeness to him, like he's family of some sort, and I feel for him. I just noticed that Rocking Man is wearing one blue sock and one black sock. I don't think he's aware of it. I've done that and I was mortified to see the mistake I'd made. He doesn't know or he doesn't care. Then again, maybe he wants it that way. His scuffed sneakers are untied. I think it's cool that he can wear two different socks and not care.

Young Clerk backs into the waiting room and then turns around. His arms are perched in front of him with the pitchers. "Got two new pots of coffee for you," he says, smiling.

"Thank you," everyone says at the same time so that you cannot really understand the words. We just know that we are all saying the same ones, the appropriate two words.

"So sweet of you," Old Woman says.

"Yeah, thanks," Big Black Guy says.

Rocking Man is now looking at Boobs as if he's just noticed her. He's staring at what we all noticed but we held back from staring. Rocking Man is *really* staring at that chest of hers. I'm feeling a little uncomfortable for both of them. Boobs, though, is stirring her coffee and hasn't noticed the stare. And then Rocking Man speaks. I'm cringing.

"You gots big breastlies," he says. "Thems yours? I looking breastlies in magazine. Mom told me some people buy them and put on. Too compicated to me. So, where you get them? Did grow on you like that? I not seen breastlies so big."

Oh boy. Here we go. Again.

"Well," Boobs begins, "they *are* mine. I paid for them."

Rocking Man is smiling now. It's a full smile with all of his teeth showing. He likes breastlies, and I think it's cool he can say it with such freedom from whatever it is that plagues the rest of us.

"You *can* laugh," Boobs says, casting her eyes around the room and pausing on each of us. "It was meant to be funny. That Buick out there is mine because I paid for it. These are mine also because I paid for them."

So now there is a welcomed release of delayed laughter. It's sort of an unhinged type of laughter. Yes, the boobs are hers. She bought them, fair and square. That's funny. Even Sullen is chuckling now but it seems a troubled chuckle as if it's loaded with something.

"Like your breastlies," Rocking Man says. "Big. Playground bolley balls."

"Thank you," Boobs says.

We all should be able to speak so honestly.

Old Woman isn't laughing. Her gaze is focused on Sullen. Sullen isn't laughing either. Old Woman recognizes and feels some type of weight that Sullen is carrying.

"Excuse me," Old Woman says, 'but you seem so sad…like you've lost your best friend…"

Sullen looks up. Her face has that older-than-it-is, stressed look. "You're right about that," she says. She sighs and it's almost like a hiss. She tosses the magazine back onto the table.

"I'm sorry if I can't get too much into all of this fun that you guys are having," Sullen says. "The truth is, I'm angry. I'm *very* angry at every-one and angry at every-thing. I have cancer. I've had radiation. I've had chemo. This is a wig. I used to have a gorgeous head of hair, and this is what I have now. I totally hate it. I'm bald underneath.

Today I went to lunch with that best friend that you speak of, and do you know what she did? She pulled my wig off…right in the restaurant for a laugh at my expense. How's that for fun and games? How's that for the best friend logic?"

Sullen's lower lip is shaking, but she's trying to keep it still. That only makes it worse when you try to do that. She doesn't want to cry because she doesn't know any of us. No one wants to cry in front of total strangers.

"And to keep it piling on, my husband is divorcing me. So, please, just ignore me. I don't want to be in here. I didn't ask to come in here but they won't let me out of the store and I just want to go home. I only came here to buy a wrench…just a stupid, silly wrench to tighten up a stupid silly dripping faucet my stupid silly husband refused to do for me. And he took all of his stupid silly tools. Just a stupid silly wrench. One lonely wrench."

My heart is racing. I can almost feel everyone's heart racing. I'm about to throw up. Some of us are making slight guttural noises. These take the place of the words that none of us can form. There's an ache in The Waiting-Room now. A very painful, incapacitating ache. None of us can think of anything to say, anything to do, because we all know that we cannot fix this for Sullen. Who? What type of friend, what type of person would ever even think of pulling of someone's wig? But someone did.

"Excuse me," Sullen says and she's on her feet now. "I can't stay here. I have to go…I just have to get out." She has her hand on the door handle. I can see. Then she lets her hand drop to her side. Defeated. She slowly turns around. She returns to her seat and slumps back down onto it as if there isn't a drop of life left in her body.

You can feel the awkwardness in the room. I'm so uncomfortable I want to scream and run out of here. This is awful. It's uncomfortable even more so because it's all happening too fast and my emotions are spinning out of control. We are all locked down by this awkwardness. We didn't create it but, we're going to have to deal with it in some manner whether we want to or not.

Tattoos gets up from the sofa. No one is saying a word as we watch and wait it out. I don't think any of us are breathing. Tattoos moves, cat-like, with silken steps, focused and quietly, to the coffee. She pours a cup and instinctively stirs in a packet of sugar and a little cup of hazelnut creamer. She places a stirrer in the cup. She moves again, silently, and with grace, to Sullen. Tattoos doesn't say a word. She reaches her hand forward just close enough so that Sullen can see the cup without lifting her downcast head. Sullen takes the cup and nods without looking up. There is a faint smile creasing her lips and it is tugging, ever so slightly, on the rest of her face.

I feel a breath rising in my throat, almost rudely, to become a sudden gusting out but instead it eases out of me. And that's good because if it had gusted out of me everyone would have heard it. How would they react? But maybe they would have gusted too. And it feels good. I feel a tear in my eye. We all do. We all feel it. We feel something that we each identify with. We are all relieved that Tattoos did something when the rest of us were paralyzed. We knew that one of us had to say something, or do something, and we all sat there knowing that but waiting for someone else to go to her. One cup of coffee. One lonely cup of coffee. We didn't have the words. A hug wouldn't have done it. Yet, we should hug her. But she is a stranger to all of us. We are strangers to all of us. Words wouldn't have done it. We can't share this with Sullen. But a cup of coffee crossed over and made another bridge for us between different floods, between different lives. One wrench. One cup of coffee.

Crutches gets up and fills his cup. It's black coffee but he's stirring it anyway. He's not even aware, at the moment, that it makes no sense to stir a cup of black coffee. Not right now. This simple action of stirring, all caused by that uncomfortable feeling that tugs the very soul out of us. I just noticed that I'm tying my shoe. It wasn't untied. I untied it to tie it again.

"You know," Crutches says, as he's walking back to his spot on the sofa, "got a story. This one's about cows."

We all expel a huge breath at the same time. Relief. Maybe his story will make us feel better.

Eagerly, we look at Crutches. Thank heavens that someone has another story. Then we remember, sort of embarrassed, Sullen and her life. So, we all look at her almost as if we're seeking her permission, her approval, that it's okay to step into new stuff.

After another moment or two of silence, Crutches accepts the silent invite, the go-ahead sign, and says, "I don't have a fish story, but I do have a cow story."

Of course we all laugh and turn our faces to Crutches. And, at that moment, Young Clerk opens the door to our room.

"Good news for all of you," he says, "the warnings have been lifted. You are all free to go. You guys have all been so great. Thanks for not complaining. I just made more coffee so you are welcome to stay as long as you'd like. All of your cars are done. The guys just kept working out there."

We all look at him. We're so quiet I can hear our breaths. We stare at him as if he'd just delivered the State of the Union speech and we are caught up in the quandary of whether we are supposed to cheer and applaud and jump to our feet, or, if we should just continue to sit there and process what he's said.

Young Clerk puts the coffee pots down on our table in our room. He smiles and nods and mouths a thank you and out the door he goes.

And then, it's like a shock hits us that the one person in our room who hasn't said a peep and hasn't budged, is on the move. Cellphone rises to her feet. She moves slowly, almost sloth-like, still texting. She's on her way back to her kind and to the cellphone world. As she reaches to grab the door handle, she stops then pivots to face the center of the room.

"Oh, my God," she says. "Another racehorse was put down during a race."

Then she was gone. And we're left with those last words that we'll have to try to figure out what to do with.

For some reason, the rest of us are staying. But no one is *saying* that we're staying. We just do. During the tornado warning not one of us asked anyone about the storm. And we couldn't see what the storm was doing or what it looked like out there. It never occurred to us. News of the warning being lifted is an interruption, an irritation, actually. We're not ready for this to end.

CHAPTER THREE

Free to go – Free to Stay

We wanted to hear Crutches' story about a cow. But it's going to have to wait. It will *have* to wait.

"That's sad," Old Woman says, "really sad. I don't know anything about horses, but they're so pretty. And away she went and just left us like that. Never said one word the whole time until now. Strange."

"Yeah," Crutches says, "it sure happens a lot, the horses dying, I mean. They show them on TV during a breakdown with a leg all flapping around like a rag, all busted up. Sickening to see that. But maybe it's because there is so much focus on it now."

"Wish she'd stayed," Big Black says. "I'd have liked to talk to her. She was startin' to cry. Did you see?"

Now we're all paying attention to Big Black Guy. He has something to say. I think.

"My uncle worked on one of those big race horse farms all his life. Heck, wanted to be a jockey but there weren't no Black jockeys. There's still no Black jockeys, not that I know of anyway. But then look at my size. We're all big in my family. Our feet would drag," he says with a chuckle.

I'm smiling, and I'm sure everyone else is but I keep looking at Big Black Guy because I know that he has more to say and I suspect it's not going to be humorous. Still, it's a comical scene envisioning Big Black Guy, at his size, riding, and reducing the size of a racehorse down to what looks like a pony.

"My uncle used to say that the industry of the racing world began to ruin the horses when they started breedin' for beauty...beauty sells. So, they started breedin' 'em more for looks than good healthy horses with strong legs and hooves. Couple generations like that and you've lost the healthy genes, the ones with stamina and power, forever. You don't get that back. Gone for good. They bred 'em for these itty-bitty hooves and then they expect 'em to run full-tilt on 'em. And then they start 'em in hard training way too soon. Just babies when they start 'em. Still growin' and acting like babies. Bones not ready for that kind of work. People who have other saddle horses, don't even start 'em under saddle until they two, three, even four and their trainers take it really easy and slow with 'em. Look at the Olympic horses. They can be eighteen, twenty-years-old and they are in their prime and still jumpin' and dancin'. A track horse all washed up by age four, if, he even makes it that long. Then when they all washed up, they ship em' off to slaughterhouses. That's the ugly, dark side, of the racing industry nobody wants you to know 'bout. But the horses are expendable. Just breed more and run them into the ground too. And it keeps playin' over and over. Yeah. I've got lots to say."

"But it's a sport," Crutches says, "people always get hurt in sports."

"That's right. *People.* You said people. People get hurt because they choose to be in whatever sport they in. Accidents do happen to athletes. But this is only a sport for the people. Horse has no choice. The moment he's born he has no choice in what his job will be. He never gets to say what he wants to be when he grows up. Forced on him. An athlete, a person, makes a choice and that athlete can also say, 'I don't feel so good today so I'm not runnin'.' Horse can't say that and even if he's doin' his best to let his people know he don't feel so good, won't matter. They gonna pump drugs into him so he can't feel that pain. They use so many drugs on those poor horses. All that matters is they run. And they run their legs off time and again. You just buy another one or breed another one to replace it. And those legs…look how skinny and light they are and they holdin' up over a thousand pounds and forced to run on 'em. It'd be like forcin' me, all six-foot-five and 310 pounds of me, to take up ballet and stand and jump all around on my one big toe. Somethin's gonna break. Yeah, horses love to run and that's part of the beauty. People say that they love to run in the races. Of course, they're runnin'…look how they whipped, man. Who wouldn't run from it? If they love it so much then there'd be no need for whips. The whips also keep that horse from slowin' down because he knows something's wrong in his body and that he needs to stop. Jockey not listenin' to that. That jockey gonna whip on him more if he starts to slow down. They force lame horses to run when they shouldn't be walking let alone runnin'. They need to heal and sometime those injuries should never be okay for them to race. There're races where every single horse is doped silly. I have a niece in veterinary school and she did some part-time tech work at one of the tracks. She knows, and she's seen, what goes on. Can't even count the trainers and vets and owners who do doping. They pump those horses full of stuff. They use stuff like pain killers, and other drugs, both legal and not legal, you name it. And sometimes the bigger the people, the more money they have, the worse it is because they can keep folks, even veterinarians, all hushed up 'bout it. Horse havin' no choice in it either. He has no choice 'bout nothin' at all in his life. It can be a real dirty business. If it was clean why do they even have to do dope testing? All the track changes in the world not gonna fix it. The damage is done and keeps going."

Big Black Guy is shaking his head and looking at his hands as his fingers look like they are waving at the floor. I feel his anger and his pain about this for the horses.

"Those young horses," he says, still not looking up, "bring glory and money for the owners. Any time you toss in money with an animal…who you think gonna come up on the short end of the stick?"

Big Black Guy looks up and scans our faces. "It's all about money. The owners and the trainers do it for a living. They *have* to make money."

He clears his throat and slowly shakes his head again.

"Racing's been around forever and it will be around forever. Only a horse can do this. They fly on their own and they fly for us when they take us with them. Horse races probably started the first day that there were two people up on horses' backs. They can cover so much ground. So, for sure, folks gonna to want to see which horse is the fastest. But what happens on the tracks and Lord A 'Mighty what happens in the barns and sheds is plain old abuse. When a race is on TV, or even if you go watch one in person, you see only the pretty parts, the glory and the glitz.

"No one likes to learn 'bout abuse. We don't really want to know that abuse of animals, and of people, occurs. We don't want to face it. I enjoy eatin' steak but I never think about the mass sufferin' the cattle go through to give me that. The deaths have to occur but we don't think about it. We only forced to think about it when abusive treatment of those animals gets exposed. This make it safe and clean for us to keep eatin' steak."

"That's, like, a lot to digest," Lutefisk says, "pardon the pun. But it is a lot to think about. I'm not, like, going to stop eating meat. But I just don't know about the racing. I've never, like, paid that much attention to it."

"You really are an animal lover, aren't you?" Old Woman says.

"Yeah," Big Black Guy says. "You know the Bible tells us that God gave us animals to use. But nowhere does it say that He gave us animals to abuse. When money comes into the picture that's when the shortcuts come in. And whatever love for the animals that used to be there, falls away until all love for the animals is replaced with the love of success and money and the quest for more money. Dog racin', horse racin', dog fights, cock fights, circuses. Greed surely our downfall. Don't ask me what we do 'bout it. I don't have the answer. Too big for me to take on. Sorry, man. I just seen a lot. Know a lot. Doesn't sit well with me."

Our little group falls silent again. It bothers me now, and I'm guessing that it bothers the others, too, considering what people will do to make a buck. But will I think about the racehorses tomorrow or the next day? Probably not. I will go on thinking about and doing the things that are my own, the things that are important to *me*. That's what we'll all do. It would be easy to conclude that humans, by nature, are greedy and selfish. So, will I be selfish if I don't at least think about the racehorses tomorrow? I suppose I don't care if I am. None of us care about things that don't personally affect us. It can further wreck your day when you learn about something you never knew occurred. It can stun. How we deal with it—is to do nothing with it. But I suppose it stuns some people into action. I wonder if Cellphone is more involved in the horseracing abuses than just hanging onto her phone and leaving folks with a few parting words before she walks out of a door?

Already, I'm thinking that we really need to hear another story from one of us. Almost as if cued to do so, Sullen looks at Crutches. She smiles. She smiles her first smile since she's been in The Waiting-Room. I think it might be her only smile of the day. This could be her fist smile in a few weeks.

"How about that cow story?" she says.

So, now it will be cows. Here we go. Of course, cows were just on my mind.

"Okay, okay," Crutches says. "I'll tell you. This was a few years ago. My sister and I were driving home from a gig," he says, "we sing. That night coming home we took all back roads. It was dark and really cold with a negative wind chill and lots of snow and ice everywhere, but I don't remember what time it was. We were out in the country, all farm land, though we couldn't see much but darkness and fences. I stopped at this four-way stop corner, and we both looked over into a fence and saw three cows just staring us down. They have those huge, soulful eyes…cows do, you know, cows have these big eyes. We sat there for a few minutes and we both decided that those cows didn't have any water, and that's why they were staring at us. They were trying to convince anyone who stopped at the corner to get them some water. I pulled on through the stop sign. I went about fifty feet and slowed down. 'You're going back, aren't you?' My sister said. 'Yep,' I told her. 'But how are we going to do this?' She asked. I grabbed the flashlight that was rolling around on the floor of my van and got out. The light hit on two of those big white five-gallon pails near the fence but on the other side of the fence from the cows. Across the street was a church. We had been so worried about the cows we hadn't noticed the church, all lit up, because they were having a Wednesday night service. We could hear a piano and singing as we crossed the road with the pails in hand. 'We can't disturb them,' my sis said. 'But those cows have gotta have water and those people are busy in the church with their service. They won't notice us,' I said. We looked all around the outside and couldn't find a faucet. So, we tip-toed inside the church. 'What if they catch us,' she said, 'and we mess up their service? What if it's a funeral?' 'They sound pretty happy to me,' I said and told her that if we got caught, we'll just say we're sorry and leave. So, I opened up the back door of the church and we both went down into the basement. And there was a faucet. We filled the buckets up and hauled them back up the stairs and across the road. I slipped through the wire fence strands, and my sister passed each heavy pail over to me. By now the cows had come over to stare at us up close, blinking those big eyes, but not moving once they got within about two feet of me. They just stared and blinked. I put each pail in the snow about three feet apart, and near them, almost right in front of the cows. The cows just continued to stare at us. They never moved. They never approached the pails. 'I guess they might be confused,' my sister said. 'They'll probably guzzle it all down once we're gone,' I said. 'They don't know us.' The whole project took us almost an hour, in the dark, in the cold. But we left the cows. We were feeling all puffed up and proud of our effort to provide water for those poor, neglected critters. So, we left and got back to town. I dropped my sister off at her apartment, and I went home. We felt pretty good about ourselves that night.

"The next day, when there was daylight, I drove back out to check on those poor neglected cows. I didn't get out of my van. Didn't have to. I saw a large pond about twenty feet into the pasture from where we'd stopped to help them. One of those cows was getting a good drink from it as I watched. She was standing up to her knees in the water.

I could see all along the edge of the pond where the cows had easily broken through the ice to get their drinks."

We all burst out laughing at that exact moment. Crutches *knew* we would.

"That's my cow story," he says, pursing his lips and grinning. Then he laughed too.

"That's so funny. It's great. One of the best I've ever heard," someone says. But I'm laughing so hard right now it doesn't matter who says what.

"It gets even better," Crutches says. He pauses just long enough to see that each of us have stopped laughing and are just about to demand that he finish the story.

"The pastor of the church owned the cows."

So now we are whooping. Old Woman is tapping both of her feet in time to her laughter. Old Man slaps his thigh. Big Black Guy tosses his head back and laughs so big-guy-like that he snorts and says he's sorry about it. Sullen is laughing. Rocking Man is Rocking.

"Like cows," Rocking Man says.

"Is that how you hurt your leg…being around cows?" Sullen asks Crutches in between her giggles.

"No," Crutches says. "I don't know anything about cows. I've never been around them except for that one night. I guess that's a real surprise to you all," he says rolling his eyes in his head as we chuckle again. The guy is funny. He knows it. I think he should take up stand-up comedy instead of singing. But that's just my opinion. I've never heard him sing.

"My next-door neighbor came over to return my generator… he's a cop…anyway I don't know why but my dog decided to yank me off the steps. I had just put his leash on and away we went. We went to the hospital. It's a really, really bad sprain, but I can put some weight on it now," Crutches says.

Everyone is murmuring at the same time now about the various sprains and breaks we've had over the course of our lives. I think we do this to identify with someone because we don't know what else to say. Probably just a simple, 'oh' would do but we jabber on far longer. People always feel they need to say something. We have to join in and find a place of commonality. I think. It reminds me of the scene in the movie, *Jaws*, when Matt and Quint are comparing their shark wounds in an effort to have the most-revered story and the most-revered scar. But the scene in The Waiting-Room probably isn't one of one-upmanship. I think we just want to feel included. We want to feel like we are part of a group.

"Now that's, like, a tough job," Lutefisk says, "being a cop."

"Yes. It is," says the athletic looking lady. She hasn't said much at all during our tornado confinement.

"I'm a police officer," she says.

"Well you certainly don't look like the big bruisers I grew up seeing," Old Woman says.

"That's impressive," Lutefisk says. "Like, how long you been at it?"

"Nine years," Cop Lady says. "I was put back on the road a week ago because I came out of working undercover in narcotics."

"Wow," Crutches says, "that's gotta be *really* tough. Isn't it?"

"Yes," Cop Lady says, "parts of it are."

"I stop by police all time," Accent says. "Pizza place guy say I stop for driving Brown because skin brown."

Oh boy. Here we go. Again.

Big Black Guy flashes a knowing-type of subtle grin. He doesn't have to say, and doesn't say, "I know what you mean." Still, I don't fully understand his expression. I don't know how to read it. I can only guess, because I'm not Black. Is he amused and thinking that Cop Lady is full of crap? Is it a smirk of anger? Was he thinking that it's about time one of us, of the white crowd, speaks up? Or was it none of that and he's just pleasantly surprised? I don't know. Someone should ask him. But no one will.

"I won't lie to you or say that it doesn't happen. The racial pro-filing and stopping does happen." Cop Lady says. "Lots of bad things happen. It's always been that way, and I don't know if it will ever change. The difference now is that we have cellphones that can capture the abuses of power. Those who abuse the power they've been entrusted with can get caught in the act. But it doesn't change what that officer feels or thinks. The possibility of getting caught shouldn't be the reason that people behave and act appropriately. They should not do the racial profiling, or the abuses of power, because it's wrong, not just because you might get caught. But it continues to happen. Sometimes adrenaline overtakes someone's thoughts, and people get too worked up, and they act without thinking. And then when it's all over, *then* they think, my God, what have I done? And it's too late by then even though the whole thing took just seconds. Maybe there aren't enough of those seconds or minutes for people to reengage their thinking. That adrenaline takes over and overrides whatever training had been there. And with that surge of adrenaline the real you and what you truly believe gets exposed."

Now I'm wondering, does the racial-profiling exist within me too? I'm remembering that the first person I noticed when I came in this room was Big Black Guy. Where do I stand with this? Why was Big

Black Guy the first person I noticed? I'd like to say it was because he's big. He takes up a lot of room. But if I want to be honest with myself, Old Man and Old Woman take up more space. Size might not have had anything to do with it. I believed that Accent was a terrorist. How do I know that? I don't. But, just like the racehorses, I'm probably not going to think about this tomorrow. Then again, maybe I will. Maybe I should. Really. Maybe that's the piece that's missing and that could lead to healing?

"Well," Old Woman says, "like that saying that there is good and bad in everyone. I guess that's true. I want to believe that there are more good police officers than there are bad ones."

"I wonder, like, what the answer is to all of it?" Lutefisk says.

"I don't know," Cop Lady says. "I truly don't know. I'd be famous and everyone would flock around me to hear me speak if I had even part of the solution. I don't have the answers. There are tons of good, decent cops and then there are those few I'm ashamed of. Racism runs so deep it's like we need a transfusion to get it gone."

Cop Lady pauses and then says, "All lives *do* matter. It's just that we're not all treated the same because of our color. That's the issue. It's not the same for everyone."

Now we are all reasonably uncomfortable again, hit with something that yanks within ourselves and jerks all words from our brains. We once again don't know what else to do. But we still have no plans to leave. Everyone is shifting their bodies around. Crutches leans up half-standing and grabs a cookie and the rest of us do the same. Just like wild turkeys we follow a leader no matter where he's headed or what he does because that equals security. That lone bird out front doesn't even know how to be a leader but we're going to follow him anyway. I guess it helps to convince us that we really do have a purpose and maybe a reason for being and that somehow, we are all of the same species.

"Red birds. Birthdays," Rocking Man says and returns to humming.

We all look at Rocking Man. I have no clue what any of us are thinking. I have no clue what I'm thinking. But I feel like I just got hit with a stone, just a pebble maybe, but sometimes you feel a pebble more than a boulder. Something hit me, pinged me. Someplace. There is a weighted silence. Something just occurred but there isn't one of us who knows what that is.

"I guess since we're all stuck here together telling our stories, I'll tell you mine," Cop Lady says.

Now all of us are studying her. We are studying her face, her eyes, and we all glance at each other. We want to hear the story. We all are being reeled into her. Willingly, we go.

"Not everyone will understand this…but maybe some of you will."

Now we are riveted to her. Waiting. Silent.

"Not a whole lot I can tell you about how the narcotics division works. I have to keep that just among cops. So, bear with me. In the department where I work, we can ask to be in narcotics and it's usually a two, or, three-year stint that you get, and then they move you out. The logic is that it can be too stressful. You're acting the whole time you are undercover. You get issued a fake name and fake ID, and we never work in the city where we normally work, or live, so it can be half the state away. The object in narcotics is to get information from someone who's been arrested and wants to rollover information to us for a lesser charge or, whatever, can be worked out. That's the snitch you've probably heard about. We want the snitch to turn us on to other drug dealers...those who are bigger fish in the pond so-to-speak.

"I had one snitch who wanted to introduce me to another dealer. A woman. My age. When my sergeants arranged for me to meet her through another informant, she impressed me. She was very attractive and dressed beautifully. She made a lot of money in her real job but also in drugs. Cocaine. Anyway. It was set up that I had what we called the 'hello phone.' It's another phone that rings to my fake name and ID. During my work shift I'd make arrangements with her before me and the team would drive to her location and I'd go visit her at her work place and have a drink with her. When you are working undercover, you can have a drink as part of your cover. Every now and then she would turn me on to another dealer and we'd make our buys and gather evidence. She also called me about other things. She confided in me about the men in her life, her family troubles, and other things that concerned her. She called me when her beloved cat died. I'd listen, as any friend would, and offer advice if I felt so moved. I'd listen and when we hung up, I'd go on about my own business, not thinking anything at all about those personal conversations of hers. Those conversations were part of my job. And it was my job to be a fake person. This went on for months and then finally my superiors decided that it was time to make some busts, arrests, and she would be included. They shut down a work when no upward movement is happening and when they think that the undercover officers are at risk of being burned, found out to be narcs, that is. Normally, the undercover officer isn't part of the arrests so that your identity is secure. But on the night that they arrested her, I just so happened to walk by the office at her work place where they had her detained and were interviewing her. The door was open and she saw me. I had to stop to talk to one of the sergeants. My eyes met hers. Her eyes immediately filled up with tears and she began to shake.

She said, 'You?' Then she burst into sobs. I turned and walked away. I found a chair away from everyone and sat by myself for a long time. It was an awful experience and it felt like a train had slammed into me. And I realize…not everyone will understand this…I mean she was a drug dealer…and that's bad…and she had to be taken down…but not once in my life, until that time, had I ever shafted a friend. And it hit me, then, that while I was acting and gathering evidence…it was *real*…for her. The friendship was real. She never thought about us as being drug dealers. She only perceived me as her best friend. And it was all fake. I did my job and I did it well. The *job* was real to me. The *friendship* was real to her. Not sure if folks can understand all of this, and I guess that doesn't matter."

Cop Lady sits with her hands entwined on her lap. Her eyes remain down. She doesn't have to look up for the pain to grab onto each of us. She's right. I don't think we understand the cop part of it but we all understand the power and the intimacy of friendship. We've probably all been shafted by a friend we loved and trusted. I know I have been. And we know what that sting feels like. You remember it forever, and it changes you forever too.

I want to say something, anything, but don't because I'm afraid it will come out wrong and that I'll only sound stupid. We are all thinking this and hoping, *somebody, please, say something.* We feel uncomfortable that Cop Lady is just sitting there with a room full of people around her yet she's totally alone with this.

"But…" Tattoos says, "we all understand empathy? We all understand compassion?"

Cop Lady nods. "Thanks," she says.

I see that Cop Lady's story resonates with Sullen. Sullen looks preoccupied as she's surely replaying the crappy scene that she tried to live through earlier that day with *her* so-called best friend pulling her wig off. Sullen is so quiet, so statue-like she doesn't quite fit in to this moment. She must be thinking, *no, we don't all understand empathy and compassion.*

"Sweetie," Old Woman says to Cop Lady, "sweetie, look at me."

Cop Lady lifts her eyes to Old Woman's eyes.

"It's a real gift to be able to feel for another person, regardless of what they've done, and that makes you special. You did your job but you are still able to see the human part of it even though it doesn't change what you feel you did to her."

"Thanks," Cop Lady says.

"I wish we had more cops like you," Big Black Guy says. "I don't usually hear that level of compassion from a police officer."

"Yep?" Tattoos say.

"So, where do you go from here in police work?" Crutches asks.

"My husband is also in law enforcement," Cop Lady says, "and he's been offered a teaching position in criminal justice out of state. So, we're moving and I've already been hired by another agency."

"That all sounds positive," Old Woman says.

"Yeah. I think we're ready for the change," Cop Lady says.

Sullen stirs and makes a slight, fake cough, the kind we make to let others know that we want to speak. She coughs again.

"I know that there are also funny things that happen with cops," Sullen says. "I have a funny story to tell you."

We all want to hear something funny, anything light, especially if it's from Sullen. We all want to make amends for what her friend, another human, subjected her to.

"I think we need another funny story right 'bout now," Big Black Guy says.

"Okay," Sullen says. "This happened about eight years ago. I was coming home from the laundromat with my basket of clothes on the front seat next to me. I had a different car then...a little wreck that I had to drive to and from classes and around town. I knew the car had a taillight out, but I didn't think too much about it. That day when I was coming home from the laundromat, I look in the rearview mirror and, yep, there is a police car behind me with his lights on. I pulled over right away. I knew he would ask me for my license and proof of insurance and registration and I wanted to be prepared. Got my license out of my purse and then leaned over to get the other stuff out of the glove box. Rolled the window down just as the officer approached. I had my nicest, biggest smile on and said, 'hello, officer.' He stopped dead. Nothing about him moved at all and he just stood there staring at me but I noticed that his eyes seemed to be kind of twitching. And he smiled, sorta caught his breath, and then smiled again. 'Do you know,' he started and then I could swear he was trying to keep from bursting out laughing. That made me feel really bad. I mean, why was a cop laughing at me? He composed himself and finished saying, 'You have a tail light out. Did you know that?' I told him I knew about that and that I would get it fixed and I asked him to please not give me a ticket. He smiled again and handed me back my stuff. 'No ticket,' he said. 'You have a good day.' And then he walked back to his patrol car. I sat and watched him in the mirror and I could that he was laughing and laughing. I could see he had the microphone thing in his hand and was talking to someone on that but I could tell that he had to keep stopping and starting because he was laughing so much. All I could see were his teeth over and over as he kept laughing. My face was hot and I was just about in tears. Then his car started to move around me and I just kept looking down so I didn't have to see him laughing at me. Maybe he'd wave at me and laugh at the same time. So, I started to cry. I cried because the cop laughed at me and I cried because this was a big deal. It was the first time I'd ever been stopped by a cop. I knew mascara would be starting to run so I grabbed a towel from my laundry basket and looked in the mirror. Then I saw it. I had my sexiest, skimpiest, red lacy thong underwear dangling from my right earring. When I leaned over to get my stuff, I snagged the panties on the earring from the laundry basket."

We all burst in to whoops of laughter at the exact same moment. It's the funniest story I've *ever* heard.

Old Woman is stomping her feet again and tossing her head back. "Oh, you didn't," she says.

"Oh, yes, I did. Yep," Sullen says.

"I wish I'd been that cop or at least been a mouse in the back of your car or the back of his car," Big Black Guy says, in between his big laughs.

Old Man is snorting. He's making little wheezy snorts of laughter.

Cop Lady is laughing. "That stuff really does happen," she says. "I could tell you lots of stories too."

"I had to drive away, no, I had to like, slink away," Sullen says. My face was the color of a tomato and it was hot to the touch. I was *so* embarrassed I could barely breathe let alone drive. I was only twenty-three at the time and I was so horrified and so worried that I'd run into that same cop again. I got the tail light fixed the next day so that I wouldn't get stopped by any cop. He probably told everyone."

"Yes," Cop Lady says, laughing, "he did."

"It is hilarious, isn't it?" Sullen says. "At least now it is. But at the time it was the worst experience of my life. I was embarrassed to even buy the thongs to begin with, but all my girlfriends had them so I wanted to be like them. Could only happen to me."

The door to our room opens and Young Clerk pokes his head in. "I heard all this laughter," he says, "and I just have to know what's going on?"

"Don't nobody tell him," Sullen says, cautioning us by flicking her index finger back and forth.

"This girl right here," Big Black Guy says, "she got stopped by the police with a…and she had a thong underpants stuck to her earring."

Young Clerk's eyes flash to Sullen. We are all laughing again, so rowdy and staccato-like that we can't speak. Sullen is nodding, red-faced and laughing at the same time. Young Clerk starts to laugh too but then realizes that he doesn't quite know why. So, he ducks back out of the room. He would've loved to join in the fun but he missed out on the whole story so he must feel confused, uncertain, and left-out. That's how I would feel. It's no fun trying to join on-going laughter that started eons before you walked into it.

After Young Clerk leaves, our laughter downshifts to a few sighs and smirks.

"Storm done," Rocking Man says. "Mom soon come I go."

"Excuse me," Old Woman says to Rocking Man, as she composes herself, "you said you came to the store to look for red birds. What does that mean?"

"Don't know red birds?"

"No. I'm not sure what you mean."

"*Birds*…red," Rocking Man says with a frown that screams "how stupid can you be?"

"Don't know red birds," Rocking Man says, "open eyes."

"Do you mean cardinals? *Those* red birds?"

"Yepper. Same. Birds red. Name too big. Red bird better. They red."

"How would you find red birds here?"

"Sometime store sell red birds. In dishes."

Now we get it. Rocking Man collects cardinal figurines.

"How many you got?" Big Black Guy asks.

"Three hunert and forty and two," Rocking Man says. He is smiling and very proud of his birds.

"How did you get interested in red birds?" Sullen asks. "I think they're very pretty too."

"When little boy I on swing at school. Boy call me 'retard.' I fall off swing and ran and ran and ran. I cry and cry and cry. Sat on step. I cry and cry and cry. Look by me and red bird by me, right *here*," Rocking Man says, as he places his right hand about three inches from his thigh.

"Red bird sat with me. I no cry. God send me red bird."

The Waiting-Room door pushes open and in walks a woman. She's wearing glasses but I can see that she has a concerned look on her face as she scans the room.

"There you are," she says to Rocking Man who is shuffling across the room to get to her. He's smiling. He's always smiling.

"Mom," he says. He drops all of his back packs and objects and hugs her. The pile of cookie crumbs gathered on his chest sprint to the floor.

"Okay, okay," she says. "Get your stuff and we'll get home. Did you find any red birds?"

"Noper. Not today. These new friends."

"Thanks," the woman says, glancing at each of us. My son collects red bird statues in case he hasn't told you. Thanks for being his friends during the storm."

"Bang, bang, bang, bang, bang," Rocking Man says, "red birds and birthdays. That it." And then he was gone.

And poof, here is that moment of silence that we seem to encounter a lot in The Waiting-Room. I don't know what we are feeling or thinking. I have no clue.

"Nice fella," Big Black Guys says. "Kinda feel sorry for someone like that. Makes you wonder why someone is born like that."

"But he doesn't know he's any different. Really," Sullen says. "He didn't like being called a name. But other than that, he really doesn't know he has a disability. He's happy. He's probably happier than the rest of us. He's certainly happier than *me*."

"This is true," Big Black Guy says. "I stand corrected. "Wonder what he meant when he said all the bang, bangs?"

"He doesn't look like someone who knows much about guns, let alone carries one," Crutches says. "I hope not anyway."

"At least we got a police officer here to protect us," Big Black Guy says. "Do you carry off-duty?"

"Yes," Cop Lady says. "We have to."

"I understand that *you* have to carry one. But they still scare me," Old Woman says.

"But they have their place," Old Man says, "such as in war or in police work."

"And," Crutches says, "It *is* our Constitutional right to carry them."

"I have always thought?" Tattoos says, "that men who carry a concealed weapon are really only doing it because they just want a bigger dick?"

Oh boy. Here we go. This is going to get downright rugged.

"But women carry too," Crutches says.

"Well…then I guess that means that a woman…"

"Oh don't even go there," Sullen says.

This is one of those times when everyone has an opinion, but they will leave the conversation to those few who are passionate enough, or stupid enough, to forge on with their rambling. The rest of us will listen and watch back and forth much like you'd watch a tennis match. Everyone has an opinion but we seek to express those opinions with those of like-mind and opinion. We ease into a topic, testing, checking to see if we are on familiar turf. We're never seeking resolution to the topic or the dilemma. What we want is validation. We don't really want to fight about it. Do we? Some folks, however, want to initiate, and keep up with, the drama. I'm guessing that they do so because they know they are going to leave those who are watching and listening. They'll never see the person again, so, it's safe. And, we might hold back because we don't know how long we're going to be with someone.

"You know the mass shooting last week at the restaurant?" Lutefisk says.

We all swivel our heads at that serve and then immediately swivel again all around the room as we try to figure out who will chime in next. I hope no one gets hurt in this game. But Lutefisk continues.

"My seven-year-old daughter was injured in that mess..."

"Oh, I am so sorry to hear that," Old Woman says as she reaches out her hand as if in an effort to maybe give a hand-hug of some type. "Is she okay? Was she shot?"

"She's, like, physically okay," Lutefisk says. "And no, she wasn't shot. She'd gone to the restaurant for a friend's birthday party. When the shooter came in and started spraying bullets, she was trampled by people running for safety. She did get a broken wrist. But it's, like, the mental scars and the emotional scars of the ordeal that's for keeps. She's not my same little girl. I don't think she'll ever be the same happy little kid I used to see playing on her swing in the backyard and playing with her Barbies. She hardly ever goes outside anymore. She mostly clings to me and her mom, to her mom, especially now. She's, like, afraid to get in the car to go anywhere. I don't know if we can ever get her to a restaurant again."

"Oh, wow," Accent says. "Horrible. Horrible bad for little kid go through and dealt with."

"The wife and me got her in to see a counselor," Lutefisk says, "but she, like, won't talk to the counselor. She just sits there. I don't think she knows how to express her feelings. But we're hanging in there."

"I'm so sorry," Crutches says. "That's why we do need concealed weapons in all public places. The only thing that stops a bad guy with a gun is a good guy with a gun. The saying goes something like that. People need to carry them to protect themselves and others."

"I'm not so sure I agree with that," Lutefisk says. "Think about our friend who collects the red birds. Do we, like, want him to carry a loaded pistol?"

So now we sit, souped-down by our own thoughts and apprehensions about speaking. We all want to be perceived as right, or, we want to be safely included in the majority, but first we have to figure out what that is.

"Yeah," Crutches says, "I don't really want him to have a gun, but it's his right to have a gun."

"Just because it's a right doesn't always mean it's something you should do or should be able to do. It's legal to smoke pot but I'm not going to smoke it."

"But it's *your* choice," Crutches says.

Cop Lady puts down the magazine she'd picked up when this conversation started. It seemed like she didn't want to get involved. Probably a police thing that they aren't supposed to talk politics or controversial things. Then again, it might just be her choice to stay out of things that can get ugly.

Cop Lady just looks straight ahead, as if she doesn't want to put anyone on the spot, like she doesn't want to draw attention to herself and her own emotions and thoughts. But she has something to say. She feels compelled to speak.

"At that very shooting," she says, "five people were shot. Two were killed. There were at least that many other injuries, as you have heard. There were three regular citizens in the restaurant at the time who had concealed weapons on them. With them. They all ran with everyone else for safety."

Silence.

Until this time in our stay in The Waiting-Room, we've heard about fish, marriage, parents, dancing in the snow, and friends but not a blurb was uttered about this most recent mass shooting. Maybe it took until now for us all to feel comfortable enough in a room full of strangers to bring it up. And you never really expect that someone next to you had been personally and intimately impacted by whatever the tragedy happens to be at the moment.

Old Man clears his throat. He runs both hands down his thighs and back up tighter onto his lap. "Some of you are a little too young to remember this," he says, "but I do. Years ago, when you heard that someone had cancer it was met with an open-mouthed gasp. We were terrified to even hear the word let alone speak it. And nowadays, it's so common, it touches everyone's life in some manner. You either have or have had cancer or you have a family member who does, or a good friend. It's so commonplace that we are so used to it. It doesn't shock us the way it used to. I think the mass shootings are the same way. We've become used to them happening and though we still feel sad and powerless and uncertain in the face of cancer and with the shootings, we can't *do* anything to avoid them. We never know when either is going to hit. So, I think our minds find ways to gloss them both over. It might be self-preservation. I don't know," Old Man says. "Just my thoughts anyway."

Sullen's left leg is crossed over her right leg. She's twitching her left foot in up and down, in round about little circles. Our eyes meet. There is a frown in her eyes but it skipped over her face. But I can see the frown in her eyes. She won't say anything. What *could* she say? I feel like crap. We all do I'm sure. Sullen knows—cancer *still* stings and *still* wrecks lives.

Suddenly, the bugle call of the Kentucky Derby blasts out. We're all bobbing our heads around trying to discern its location and the reason for the loud interruption.

"S'cuse me," Accent says. "My phone."

Accent takes his cellphone out of his jacket pocket. "Yes," he says. He's smiling and looking down at his shoes. He reaches down to flick a piece of grass off one shoe. "Yes, I safe. When get home. Yes, we go looking wild barkins. Yes. Bye-bye."

Accent puts his phone back in the pocket. "My son," he says and nothing further.

So, do Accent and his son go looking for wild *dogs*? I mean, what *is* a wild barkin?

Of course, leave it to Old Woman to ask.

"Excuse me," she says, "but what is a wild barkin?"

Accent flicks his eyes to her with a puzzled look on his face. He wants to say, "What? You don't understand English?" I think. But he doesn't. Instead, he says, "Bar…kins," as if we know now what they are. "You know," he says, "kins…with bar in them? Kins, that people toss out car window on road?"

No doubt that everyone of us, just like me, is stuck in perplexity now. We are trying to make sense of this. No one wants to insult Accent but we haven't a clue what he's talking about.

Old Man speaks. "By chance do you mean *beer cans*?"

"Yes, yes," Accent says, delight spilling out with his words that someone finally got it. Someone grasped the vocabulary lesson for the day.

"My son," Accent says, laughing, "he ten. Love to go out on road and search for the kins. Gets money for them. Wants to buy bye-cycle when has more."

We all bust out laughing. It's a safe thing to do because Accent is laughing too. We could have offended him if we'd jumped into the laughter too soon. I didn't laugh at Zucchini Baby and I didn't laugh at the barkins too soon. So, I'm proud of me. But I'm laughing now.

"My English...still not best," he says. "Here in Amereeca a time but still not best. Funny. First week here I take son to store to find...a place to...well to find place. I went to nice lady at desk and ask, 'where is saloon? Take son saloon.' She go like this, lean way forward to look down on son...three. He three. She make ugly face at me and shake head. She no say no more. Took son out of store and ask other lady where is saloon for son. She ask why take son to saloon? Not what done here Amereeca. I said boys have hair cut here. She look at me like this, squinty and then smile, 'You mean *salon*?' I tell her yes, yes, saloon, place of haircut."

Lordy are we laughing now. Hysterically. So is Accent. He knows the story is funny and I'm sure he's told it many times whenever his English causes confusion. This time, it was the wild barkins to blame and provide Accent his cue.

The Bobbleheads are all nodding again and we're all sighing a comfortable sigh. We seem to be winding down. It's getting quiet again. A different kind of quiet.

I notice that everyone one-at-time either looks up at the large institutional-looking clock on the wall, or, looks at a wristwatch. Oddly, I've never even noticed the big clock before and I don't think anyone else has either. When people start looking at clocks and watches it means the end has come.

CHAPTER FOUR

Time to Go

And so, the storm has ended. The day has ended. It's time for us to part and return to our own lives.

As each person stands up to leave The Waiting-Room, we look at each other for the last time ever. There is always that hesitation when we're about to say goodbye. The hesitation is just a tad longer with people who are strangers but with whom you've shared…*something*. But we are still strangers, all of us, and we will never see each other again. So, what *do* you say?

"It's time to leave," Old Woman says. "We can all go home now. I've enjoyed sitting here with all of you. I've enjoyed sharing our stories. We sure discussed a lot of things. But it's time to go home."

"Have good and full lives," Old Man says as he opens the door that will take him and Old Woman to the counter to pay for the tires and service and collect their keys. The same door will take all of us back to our responsibilities and personal interests.

"Enjoy that honeymoon," Crutches says as he hoists himself up onto his crutches and then he is the next one to aim for the door. Big Black Guy jumps up and grabs the door for Crutches and they walk out almost together. But as soon as they are away from the desk, they will separate and each will go his own way.

Crutches calls out, "See you later."

I catch myself with a half-grin. No, there won't be a "later". None of us will ever see each other again. That's how this works. That's how it will stay. One-by-one they all go. And then everyone's gone.

I'm the only one still sitting here in The Waiting-Room. I'm pleased that I can go home. I also have a feeling of melancholy. I suspect the others felt the same mixed-up set of emotions.

I remember being on a plane once, headed for Chicago. I sat next to a young guy who told me all about his having just gotten a job at a new business, fresh out of school, as a graphic designer. I was on my way to a boring conference. He rambled on about being the top of his class and then shifted to other important topics. He told me about driving a sports car and "doing a brody" and he undoubtedly picked that word to further his attempts to impress me. He continued to irritate me when he spoke of his "mum" but then explained to me, "mom" as if I couldn't decipher his lofty language. I asked him where he was from. "Pittsburg," he said, "born and raised." So much for his British facade. But I listened to him anyway. He was excited about his new life just on the verge of taking off. I was less than enthused about the boring conference I faced. But I was quite enthused about the young fella's fakery. So, I listened. Funny how we open up and talk to a stranger when you are stuck with that stranger. Funny how we sit there and listen to their ramblings when in any other situation we would have no reason to do so. We could call each other idiots and even that would be okay because we'll never see each other again. But we don't. We listen instead. Funny how this happens. The minute you leave that room, or plane, or bus, your own reality greets you at the exit.

And now, here I sit. I'm thinking that the only regret is that we should have hugged. But we held back. It seems we always hold back because we are supposed to, or, because we think the other person will think poorly of us. I don't know. But something feels left undone.

I see the remains and the proof that we were all together in this one room. Styrofoam cups are close to spilling over the top of a small trash can along with napkins and stirrers. There are a few coffee stains on the napkins left on the cart. There are remnants of cookies on the plate, all made of the same stuff, thrown together on the same plate. Some whole, some broken, but all made of the same cookie dough and fillings.

There is one cookie left on the plate. It's quirky how no one ever takes that last cookie. We *never* do. A person could have robbed a bank that morning, but he won't take that last cookie.

Nameless people. We'll never see each other again yet we'll remember each person somewhere in those deeper jars of memories that we all keep but seldom open again. But they're there. And they add something. They were important at the time because we had nothing else to do and because we each had that ominous thought recurring, *what if I'm going to die?* We'd been herded in here and plunked into this room for the same reason until we became a closed group. All different people, all different lives, different experiences and ages, but in the same room for the same reason. While we waited for our vehicles a tornado could have blasted us all gone. So, we chatted. I think we spew just enough to come clean with a few things, not so much for the others, but for ourselves, holding back just enough and being decent with each other because, who knows? At any moment we might be standing in front of God. Time needs to pass before we can comfortably return to saying things that we know will rile people up. The time needs to pass, so that, hopefully, God forgets about it or it's no longer new enough to matter to Him. Yet, these people and the conversations are no longer important enough that we'll tell anyone else once we are free of The Waiting-Room and we've safely returned to our lives and plans and callings. We'd been here together long enough that a common comfort sprouted and we could tip-toe onto controversial terrain without us punching each other out or walking off in a huff. Funny how we start out being on our best behavior. But that can only last so long for us humans and then the real us begins to emerge through it all and starts to gain some ground and become visible. Kind of like a little mole in your yard. One little creature smaller than your hand and he can chip away and chip away at dirt until you look back at where he's been and marvel at the vast distance he's covered. This reminds me of the saying about the honeymoon phase. I'm not so sure I like the honeymoon phase or if I like the raw reality the best. It could be that the honeymoon phase has to exist to lead us into reality so that we aren't shocked to the extent that we flee humanity entirely.

From raccoons to shrimp. How do we make it? How do there get to be so many things and so much stuff on this planet for us to delve into? How do we find it all? How do each of us find our chunk of turf and know when and for how long to dig in? How does that little mole choose *your* yard? How do you end up being a lutefisk person or a nurse? How do you end up being a dog person or a man who hunts for wild barkins? How do we make it? How do we end up being so different and still make it through our days?

So many things link us, coffee and cookies, moms and dads, love and lost love, and things like cancer and death. So much about life and our experiences find ways to link us even though it might not have been something we've set out to do, or, something we've each chosen. I suppose this helps us know we are real and that we really do exist. It helps me know I am me.

There are lots of routes for us to choose and still so many choices left to make. Things seem to be predestined, or chosen for us, as if we really don't have any choice in them, such as, what country you are born in. I hope we do have some chances to make the choices and that we only want to blame fate or blame God when we make the wrong choice.

Bubble-wrap makes us happy. New stuff makes us happy. And maybe it truly can best be summed up in red birds and birthdays. That might be the answer to all of it—an innocent and simple view of life.

I'm not bummed anymore about there not being any bubble-wrap left for me. I'm not bummed anymore about shelling out so many bucks today on an old beater. I'm going home.

I'm walking across The Waiting-Room and as soon as I get out of the building, nice new tires are waiting to take me wherever I need to go. My hand is on the door handle. But before I open the door, I stop. I turn around and take a sweeping view of the empty room. I want to save this picture somewhere stored in my mind but I don't know why. This is a room I will probably never see again. And, even if I do return at some time in the future, it won't be the same.

My eyes fall to the cart and that one last cookie.